B

AFTER THE STORM

Following the death of her father and an unhappy love affair, Ashley Elliott goes to Yorkshire to live with her sister. She also hopes to find the peace and tranquillity that is missing from her life. Instead, she meets Brad Thornton, a man of a brooding and often hostile nature, who makes no secret of the fact that he dislikes her. When she finds she is falling in love with him, Ashley sets out to unravel the mystery that surrounds Brad Thornton.

AFTER THE STORM

After
The Storm

by
Marlene E. McFadden

Dales Large Print Books
Long Preston, North Yorkshire,
England.

British Library Cataloguing in Publication Data.

McFadden, Marlene E.
    After the storm.

    A catalogue record for this book is
    available from the British Library

    ISBN 1-85389-816-3 pbk

First published in Great Britain by Robert Hale Ltd., 1992

Published in Large Print 1999 by arrangement with Robert
Hale Ltd.

Dales Large Print is an imprint of
Library Magna Books Ltd.
Printed and bound in Great Britain by
T.J. International Ltd., Cornwall, PL28 8RW.

One

Ashley finally decided to move up North after her last disastrous evening with Karl.

Her sister Andrea had been begging her to leave London ever since their father had died nearly six months before. Ashley remembered that time well. The tearful, yet joyful reunion with her older sister after a two-year parting; the apologies they had made to one another because, of course, they had always intended to meet more often; the remembrances, happy and sad, that they had shared. On that occasion, too, Ashley had met Andrea's brand new husband, a tall, young and very likeable Anglican vicar who had recently been promoted from curate and taken over a small country parish. Ashley had teased her sister about being married to a vicar, but Andrea and her husband, Peter, had taken it all in good part, and were so admirably suited to one another and so obviously deeply in love that Ashley had felt pangs of acute envy. She and Karl had been seeing one another on and off for two years and had not yet taken a step towards making it permanent. Their relationship had nothing of permanence about it.

Karl travelled abroad a good deal and was never slow in reminding Ashley that she was perfectly free to go out with other men when he was away. By this she presumed he intended to see other girls. Why not? They had made no serious commitment. Ashley doubted they ever would. Karl professed to love her, but, she had to be honest, usually only when they had spent the night together. She knew he did not feel about her as she did about him. She had believed she was content with the way things were—until her father's death when Andrea and Peter came down from Yorkshire for the funeral.

'Come back with us, Ashley,' Andrea had begged her on the eve of their departure. 'I hate leaving you here on your own. And we've got lots of room. Haven't we, Peter?'

'More rooms than we'll ever need,' Peter had grinned. 'Even if we had a dozen children. You know what old vicarages are like.'

Ashley had laughed aside the invitation. 'What about my job?' she had asked, but even as she spoke she knew it wasn't the job that would keep her in the South. She was only a secretary in a bank; the sort of position she could probably pick up anywhere, given her qualifications. No, now her father, her only real link with life in London, was gone, she could understand Andrea's request. They could be close together again as they had not been since Andrea left London at the age of eighteen to go to York University. She had never gone back home again to live. Soon after finishing a three year B.A. Humanities course she had met Peter. Now she was happy and content to be a country vicar's wife, throwing any prospects of a career aside, at least for the moment. If children came along in the fullness of time, and Ashley was sure they would, she did not envisage Andrea ever taking up a career.

Ashley, on the other hand, at twenty-three had a good, well-paid job and *her* future prospects were equally good. She had a handsome boyfriend. He was fairly well off, owned his own Georgian terrace house in a fashionable leafy London square; he drove a fast sports car and was generous to a fault with worldly gifts—flowers, perfume, exciting surprises from his many trips abroad. So why did Ashley envy her sister? Why did she wish she was going back to Yorkshire with them to live in the rambling old vicarage, which probably did not have central heating or any of the smart, modern gadgets she had come to rely on? And why, perversely, did she brush aside any suggestions of going with them as though she did not really want to?

When she was alone in the flat she and her father had shared since Andrea's departure—their mother had died when they were both very young—she felt lonely and longed for Karl's return from his latest trip abroad. He had promised to phone her every day, a promise he always made and never kept. Ashley wished Karl could have been at the funeral; her father had got on well with him, but as Karl had said, 'Business comes first, love,' and she supposed he was right, but she would have liked to have felt his arm around her; she would have liked to have been comforted by him as Peter had comforted Andrea. When Karl did come back nearly a week later, Andrea and Peter had left—Karl had never even met them—and he was in such high good humour over his latest successful business venture that he did not want to know anything about the funeral and accused Ashley of trying to make him feel morbid and depressed.

That night they had had a terrible row, but the next day the inevitable red roses arrived and Karl took her out for a lavish meal. He was equally lavish with his apologies.

During the following six months, May to October, when the unending drought and hot weather made life in London unbearable, Ashley and Karl had frequent arguments. They had never had what could be called a placid relationship, but as Karl spent only odd weeks here and there in England, they had never seemed to be together long enough to get on each other's nerves. In fact, Ashley had often longed for more time with Karl. That long, hot summer, she got her wish. Karl's firm was opening a new branch in London. Karl was to be home-based for a few months to see to the smooth running of the big, plush and exclusive restaurant and private club. At first it was good. They met every day but, gradually, Ashley sensed that Karl was restless and uncomfortable. He had always been a man of action; even now he was forever coaxing Ashley to go out on the town, but she found the late nights—or more accurately, the early mornings—exhausting. If she begged him to spend an evening at home he was moody and quiet. Then he started phoning to say he could not see her, breaking their dates, often at the last minute. If it hadn't been for the still plentiful supply of gifts and flowers, Ashley would have believed he was seeing someone else, here in London, the one place where their relationship had always been sacrosanct. Once she hinted at such a possibility but Karl had laughed. Too loudly, perhaps. There wasn't another woman in his life, he assured her.

It was only a few weeks later when Ashley found out Karl had not been telling her the truth. Quite by chance she saw him crossing Trafalgar Square one lunch-time with his arm around the shoulders of a tall blonde girl. They were talking animatedly with their heads close together, Karl's so dark, the girl's so fair. Ashley made sure they did not see her and made her way unhappily back to the bank.

All afternoon she kept telling herself that the blonde girl was a business acquaintance of Karl's; that there was nothing in it; but she knew she was only deluding herself. Too many things were beginning to add up. When Karl came round to the flat unexpectedly that evening, all smiles, willing and eager to take her into his arms, Ashley said, 'I saw you with a girl today. In Trafalgar Square. Who was she?'

A slight frown creased Karl's smooth, tanned forehead. He was looking particularly handsome today in dark blue trousers and a casual, paler blue sports shirt. Ashley, as always, felt weak at the sight of him, but rigidly stood her ground.

'Girl? What girl?' His voice was curt and his eyes did not quite look into hers. His manner made Ashley more convinced than ever that this particular girl was no casual acquaintance. Karl had never shown the slightest guilt about girls he had met whilst abroad. Once when showing Ashley some pictures of a trip to Jamaica, he had been quite pleased to let her see the snaps of beautiful, bikini-clad sun-bronzed females. He had joked about them, of course, and Ashley, though feeling hurt, had never really believed herself to be threatened. Now she did.

'I saw you, Karl,' she insisted. 'You had your arm around her shoulders.'

Karl moved away from her towards the window, looking down into the street. The window was open to try to let in what bit of cool, evening air there was.

'Is that a crime?' he said.

She was going to lose him. She had never been so certain of anything in her life. She had always known that she and Karl would probably never become totally committed to one another, but the inevitable day when he would go out of her life for ever had seemed so far away; not to be really considered in any serious way.

Now, it was a very real threat. Ashley joined Karl at the window. A group of young people was strolling down on the far side of the street. Laughing, talking. On their way to the pub no doubt. Boys and girls without a care in the world. They would sit outside at a pavement table on this ridiculously warm early October night; drinking cold drinks. She envied them.

She realized with a sudden pang that she was always envying people these days. First her own sister and now a group of youngsters she did not even know. Why did other people's lives seem so much better than her own? Not more exciting. That was entirely the wrong word. Nobody could be more exciting to be with than Karl. No one could be a more wonderful lover. But Ashley wasn't looking for excitement. Then what *was* she looking for? The contentment of Andrea and Peter who walked about hand in hand wherever they went, like a couple of schoolkids? The carefree, uncomplicated freedom of the pub-going teenagers? She did not know. She was beginning to feel depressed and suddenly she wanted to have it out with Karl, to bring things to a head. She thought about the past two years of her life when Karl had been such a part of her—they had become lovers almost at once, the first man Ashley had slept with; not because she wanted a casual affair but because she loved him. She thought of the weeks and even months she had been without him, missing him, wanting only to have him back, aching for him. Two years of her life and where had it got her? Precisely nowhere.

She heard Karl begin to lie about the blonde in Trafalgar Square and with sudden, sharp, clear insight she saw him for the first time as he really was. He was handsome. He could be great fun, but she knew she wanted more, needed much more. Karl could never give her what she

17

wanted. Again, as so many times since her father's funeral, she thought about Andrea and Peter. They had so vividly described the small Yorkshire fishing village where Peter had his church that she could see it now; rough-stone cottages, steep, cobbled streets. Grey, cold sea. Hardy people; blunt and generous people who had taken Andrea and Peter, two strangers, to their hearts. If she went and lived with Andrea, if she gave up her job, took a long holiday; gave up thinking about Karl, got right away from London and memories of her father, perhaps she would find out what she truly wanted out of life—or more important still—what she could give to life.

'It's over, Karl,' she heard herself saying. She closed the window on the sounds of the street, and moved over to the settee, sitting down, waiting for him to join her as she knew he would.

'Oh, come off it, Ashley.' Karl sounded angry, striding towards her; not sitting, not trying to talk her round as she imagined he would—perhaps half-hoped he would. 'I won't see her again. She doesn't mean anything to me, anyway. I haven't known her long. If you hadn't seen us it would have died the death in time, I promise you.'

How cold he sounded. How indifferent to both Ashley's feelings and the poor blonde girl's. He was annoyed. He obviously wanted to go on seeing her, but for the life of her Ashley could not think why.

For the next hour they argued and fought each other with words. Karl offered her bribes: a holiday abroad; a trip to America if she wanted it. He was going there at Christmas. Couldn't she just imagine it—Christmas in New York? Odd that he had never offered to take her with him before. He told her he needed her. He said she was a bloody fool to want to throw away two good years. He said many things and so did she but neither of them spoke of love.

Perhaps even now, at the eleventh hour, if Karl had said, 'Ashley, I love you. Marry me. That's what I want,' or something like that she may have weakened, but he didn't. It was too late. For either of them.

At last Karl gave in, slamming out of the flat. Ashley watched him as he left the building and crossed the now dark street towards his parked car. The street lamp illuminated him. Tears filled her eyes. Was she a bloody fool as Karl had said? Surely if she loved him, and she did love him ...

But it wasn't enough. He climbed into his car and drove off, noisily, angrily. He did not look up at the window, but it was a long time before Ashley moved away to face the loneliness of her flat where only a terrible empty silence waited for her.

She moved slowly towards her bedroom. It was too early to go to bed, and she would not be able to sleep, but what else was there to do? When the telephone rang suddenly, loudly, it made her jump. She moved quickly to answer it.

'Hullo, Ashley. It's me Andrea.'

It must have been fate. A great feeling of relief flooded through Ashley. As Andrea started to apologize for not ringing earlier, Ashley was waiting eagerly for a pause in her sister's words so she could break in with, 'Andrea, can I come and live with you?'

Two

The drought broke on the day in mid-October when Ashley finally moved North. No one was particularly bothered; in fact, most were glad to see an end to the hot, sticky days and unbearable nights. The rain was refreshing and very welcome. However, once it had started to fall it did not seem to know when to stop and Ashley's first impressions of the village of Storrs were gained through pelting, wind blown rain that lashed against the windscreen of Peter's Volkswagen van, making visibility very poor. There was a heavy shroud of fog over the sea through which there loomed murky shapes of buildings and the tall, craggy cliffs in whose shadow the village stood.

Peter had insisted on driving down to

London to collect Ashley and as his van seemed to be the ideal vehicle in which to transport both Ashley and her belongings, she had accepted his offer gratefully. She had turned her back deliberately on the flat and the London street where she had lived all her life and tried to push thoughts about Karl out of her mind. She soon found that this was not as hard as she had imagined. Peter was a most amusing companion, being blessed with a quick and dry sense of humour. He was also the sort of person who was keenly interested in other people and had a wealth of funny anecdotes about people he had met in his work for the Church, all told not in any cruel or nasty way, but with genuine warmth and affection. He had another gift too, which did not become apparent to Ashley till they were well on their journey to Yorkshire. He was able to make her talk about herself without appearing to do so, and by the time they reached Storrs she realized she had talked through much of her tension and depression.

The vicarage was as she had imagined it: a large greystone house set in a fairly big and rather unkempt-looking garden very near to the church. At the moment, of course, everything was sodden and the grass, due to the drought, was patchy and brown. Scraggly bushes grew on either side of the gravel drive and there were one or two trees. The whole garden had a natural unfussy look about it which Ashley liked immediately. The inside of the house was just as unfussy, but warm and welcoming. There was a long hall of dark brown tiles, on which a gay striped rug had been placed; at the end of which the kitchen door stood open. Andrea was busy before the bright, gleaming red and black Aga cooker. She was wearing a PVC apron with a picture of Mickey Mouse on it and her curly brown hair was fastened back with a black bow. Something she was stirring in a heavy-bottomed pan smelt good. She left her stirring for a moment to come and kiss Ashley, her happiness at the safe arrival of her husband and sister showing in her face.

Peter immediately folded his arms around Andrea, nuzzling her neck affectionately. He was wearing a huge, many times washed sweater over his grey clerical shirt. At that moment, to Ashley, he looked more boy than man and the white dog collar showing above the sweater's neck seemed incongruous.

'Mmm ... smells good.' Peter released Andrea and dipped his finger in the bubbling stew, giving a little yelp at the heat of it. As he licked his finger Andrea gave his hand a playful slap.

'Peter Winford,' she scolded, 'where are your manners? Let's try to give Ashley a good first impression, shall we?'

Ashley pulled off her anorak. Peter took it and hung it on a hook at the back of the door. The wide kitchen windows beyond the sink overlooked the back garden—a mini-orchard by the look of it: pear-trees and apple-trees, some gnarled and old with well-trodden ground between them. Ashley had not yet seen much of the house but enough to know that here was a place that was meant for a big family; perhaps a dog or two. She glanced at Andrea, whose face was flushed from the heat of her cooking. Her sister would make a wonderful mother. Ashley told herself she was nowhere near as domesticated and maternal as Andrea, but in her heart she did not really believe it. Already she was deeply aware of the peace and harmony of this house; and she found herself longing to be a part of it.

Leaving Peter to continue stirring the stew, with a stern admonishment not to dare sample it, Andrea took Ashley on a brief tour of the vicarage before showing her to her room.

There was an air of general untidiness throughout, mainly caused by piles of books, books and yet more books—books on shelves, bookcases, bureaux, on the floor and balanced precariously on chair-arms. Nowhere was dirty, and fresh clean curtains hung at every window, but the presence of a thin layer of dust, the occasional shabby or worn rug or chair-covering seemed the least of Andrea's worries.

Ashley thought briefly of Karl, wondering what he would think about the place. He lived in an atmosphere of almost sterile cleanliness, a condition scrupulously maintained by his daily cleaning woman. His house gleamed and shone from top to bottom. All walls were white, furniture either black or white and with a predominance of chrome and smoked glass. When Ashley had first seen the interior of Karl's house she had been very impressed. Now she realized it was cold and soulless, that it could never be a home. Who would ever allow a dog to scramble on to those white chesterfields or have children tramp their muddy shoes across the squeaky-clean black-and-white tiled floor?

This was a real home! Where you could relax; be yourself. Eventually, after touring the breakfast-room, living-room, study, crowded, plant-filled conservatory, two bathrooms and three large bedrooms, Andrea flung open the final door on their tour.

'And this is your room. For as long as you want to stay here.'

Ashley followed her sister into the bedroom. She could not believe what she saw. There was a massive wooden fourposter bed, complete with pink canopy and bedspread. The walls were painted pink. There were rose-patterned curtains at the windows, a warm-looking deep pink carpet. All the furniture was the same dark wood as the bed. Ashley stared at Andrea. Her sister looked proud and pleased, and well she might too. The room, and especially the bed, was magnificent.

'All the furniture in here came with the

house,' Andrea explained. 'Isn't the bed something?'

'But didn't you and Peter want this bed for yourselves?' Ashley cried, going across to the bed, sitting on it. It was high and firm.

'Well ... we thought it would be nice to have this room as a guest-room. Something rather special. And as you're our first guest ...' Andrea smiled.

'Oh, Andrea!' Ashley rushed across to her sister and hugged her. 'Thank you so much. I'll never be able to repay what you've done for me.'

'Hey, none of that,' Andrea scolded gently, giving Ashley's shoulders a little shake. 'We're sisters, aren't we? Look, I'll leave you to freshen up. I'd better go and see what Peter's doing. Come down when you're ready. After supper I'll get Peter to bring your things up here.'

'You don't mind my using some of my own bits and pieces, do you?' Ashley asked anxiously.

'Honestly, Ashley, I shall hit you in a minute.' Andrea sounded quite cross. 'This is your home now. You're free to use every room, as you would in your own house, but it'll be nice, I'm sure to have your own TV and music-centre and such like.'

Ashley looked round the room again. 'And there's certainly more than enough space for all I've brought with me.'

'Of course there is,' Andrea agreed.

When she was alone, Ashley wandered over to the window. It overlooked the front of the house and through the rain and the mist Ashley had a dim vision of the coastline and the sea. The church and vicarage were situated at the top of a steep street. Now Ashley was able to look down on to the hub of the village. The houses and small slate-roofed cottages seemed to huddle together; some almost seeming to fall over one another. It was only a small place; possibly St Mark's vicarage was the largest house there was. Ashley longed to be able to explore but perhaps she ought to wait till the rain let up a bit. It would be dark soon anyway. On an impulse she flung open the window, and was surprised by the cold damp air. Perhaps it wasn't as cold as it felt, but only seemed that way by contrast with the hot weather they had been having. Now she supposed it was too much to hope that the warm summer-type weather would return. Winter would soon be here. Ashley shivered slightly as she imagined the sort of winters Storrs was probably used to. She shut the window again, but not before her nose had wrinkled appreciatively at the definite tang of the sea.

She looked around her room once more. Only two pictures adorned the walls: one above her bed, the other over the chest of drawers on the opposite wall. They were both religious pictures. The one over her bed was familiar to her though she did not know the artist—*The Light of the World*. She moved closer to have a better look. It was a large print in a gilt frame. It gave her a feeling of security. She saw it as a symbol of her future. After the last few unsettled, depressing months it was good to feel that she would have a future that would not involve Karl Whittaker. Or any other man for that matter, she decided firmly.

As she went along to the bathroom nearest to her room she felt a sudden gratitude too, because Andrea had not mentioned Karl, though both Andrea and Peter knew all about him and were under no illusions as to why Ashley had left London. As far as Ashley was concerned, Karl and London and the intricacies and impossibilities of a love life were things of the past.

Three

It was still pouring with rain the next morning, a Friday, and there seemed no sign of any let up. During the night, Ashley had kept being woken up by the sound of the howling wind and the rain lashing on the window. Despite that, she felt refreshed when she got up and more relaxed than she had in a long time. She went down to breakfast wearing a pair of jeans and a thick, dark blue sweater. The kitchen was warm and eggs were bubbling merrily in a pan on the stove. Peter was sitting by the table reading what looked like the *Church Times*.

'Good morning!' Andrea greeted her. 'Did you sleep well?'

Ashley grimaced. 'Not really. That awful wind.'

35

Peter looked up. 'Yes, I'm afraid we get a lot of that around here. We're rather exposed. Still, we're in the middle of some wonderful countryside. Scarborough's only about ten or twelve miles away. A nice place, I think, we had a very good open-air campaign there this summer. On the beach, you know.'

As he spoke Ashley could see him warming to his subject. She sat beside him at the table, prepared to listen, intensely interested in anything her brother-in-law might have to tell her, but Andrea came across with the eggs at that moment and the account of the summer campaign did not get very far. No matter, there was plenty of time. Ashley did not really consider herself to be a religious person, though both she and Andrea had been Christened and Confirmed in the Church of England, but she was willing, even eager, to become a regular church-attender. Even if she had been averse to the idea, she would have gone along to some services out of common courtesy.

'I hope you like boiled eggs,' Andrea said, scooping a fat brown egg out of the pan and popping it into a blue eggcup. 'We don't go in for big cooked breakfasts, but if you want cereals just help yourself.' She indicated the packets of cornflakes and Weetabix on the work-top. 'They're free-range eggs, of course.'

'A boiled egg will be lovely,' Ashley assured her.

Peter grinned. 'And feel free to cut your bread into "soldiers". I always do.'

It was a happy, relaxed meal. To be honest Ashley had never been a big breakfast-eater—a cup of black coffee had been all she ever wanted—now she tucked into the bread and butter and the egg, followed by two pieces of toast and marmalade, thoroughly enjoying every morsel. When she had finished, she patted her stomach and grinned.

'Gosh, if I eat like that every morning

I'm going to get fat,' she said.

'Nonsense,' Peter cried, 'you're like a reed. You could do with some meat on your bones.' He spoke like an indulgent parent. Ashley hardly knew him but it was impossible to take offence at his remarks.

She smiled. 'Now I'm not as slim as Andrea, and I never was,' she said. 'If I remember rightly she was the one who could always eat as many chocolates and cakes as she wanted and never put on an ounce.'

Peter and Andrea looked at one another. A quick glance between them, but Ashley did not miss the look in their eyes. Nor the faint pink flush that came to her sister's cheeks.

'What is it?' she asked, aware of a sort of suppressed excitement between them. Peter turned to her and before he spoke Ashley knew instinctively what he was going to tell her.

'Andrea won't be slim for long. We're having a baby in March.'

'Oh, Andrea,' Ashley leapt up from the table, gathering her sister into a warm, suffocating embrace. 'I knew you would. As soon as I got here I knew this house was made for children.'

Peter's eyebrows rose. 'Do you mind putting that in the singular, not the plural?' he pleaded.

Ashley could scarcely contain her pleasure and excitement at the wonderful news. She was suddenly filled with incredible energy and she insisted on helping Andrea with the household chores, making it clear from the outset that she was going to do her share. When the beds were made, the washing up done and the floors swept, Andrea laughed out loud, standing with her back against the sink looking at Ashley.

'Stop. Stop!' she cried. 'You're putting me to shame. We just don't go at housework like hammer and tongs in this house.'

Ashley pushed a strand of hair off her face. 'Sorry!' she said. 'It isn't really me

39

either. I was only trying to create a good impression.'

Andrea wrinkled her nose. 'It's a big house,' she said, 'and it would be a bit like painting the Forth Bridge to try to keep it all spick and span. Personally, I can think of better things to do than polishing and dusting all day long.'

'You're quite right.' Ashley put the broom away in the cluttered cupboard. 'What do you do with your time, as a matter of interest?'

Andrea perched herself on a kitchen stool. 'Well, there's the St Mark's Women's Society, the Mothers' Union, which of course I shall officially qualify for next March; there's a Sunday School class I take. I type Peter's sermons; try to keep his study in some sort of order, but I'm afraid I'm fighting a losing battle in that respect; I answer letters, visit the sick, help to clean the church, arrange flowers.'

Ashley held up her hand. 'Enough. Sorry I asked.'

They both laughed. Then Andrea spoke in a serious voice. 'I suppose you'll want to be looking for another job?'

'Well, yes, I suppose I should in a way,' Ashley admitted, 'but not just yet. There's the money Dad left me and I'd saved quite a bit. I think I'd rather just be a lady of leisure for a while, if you don't mind.'

'I don't mind in the least. I just want you to be happy.'

Ashley smiled. 'I'm happy now,' she said.

And she was. She wanted to join in all the parish activities. She wanted to be a part of everything. She wanted to meet people, make friends, become involved in any way she could. At the moment all that seemed very, very challenging and exciting.

Peter had gone over to Scarborough to visit an old lady in hospital. She was laid up with a fractured thigh and likely to be there for some time. She was one of

St Mark's longest serving parishioners and Peter made it one of his regular duties to take her Holy Communion once a week. Andrea, after she and Ashley had enjoyed a cup of morning coffee, had gone to the study to see to Peter's mail. This left Ashley at a bit of a loose end. The rain seemed to have eased off so she decided she would venture out and have a look around. She wanted to see what the village was like and for all she knew the rain might go on for days. She certainly did not want to be confined to the house all the time if it did.

Andrea let her borrow an umbrella and stood in the open front door to see her off.

'If you go to the bottom of the street and turn right you'll be in the village centre in no time and then the harbour and the beach, if you can call it a beach is only another few hundred yards. I'll see you about twelve, all right?'

Ashley waved and Andrea went back

inside. Ashley held the umbrella to shield herself from the brunt of the wind and rain and walked quickly down the drive in the direction Andrea had said. Once again she could smell the distinct tang of the sea and she began to think how nice it would be to live by the sea after spending the twenty-three years of her life in London. She had spent some holidays on the coast, of course, but never at a small fishing village. The prospect of a quiet, easy going life definitely appealed to her. She wondered briefly if Peter had chosen to begin his life as a vicar here or whether he had had to go where he was sent. He was lucky, whatever had brought him to Storrs, and so was Andrea. They could have gone to an urban parish, or an inner-city one. Surely here in this quiet place there could not possibly be any of the pressures on a young vicar that living in a town or city would produce.

Ashley soon reached the village centre. It seemed to consist of one main street, or rather hill, as it sloped downwards towards the sea. There was just a handful of small shops; a post office, a bank, general store, confectioner's and a butcher's. Neat buildings were set on either side of the street. There were small terrace cottages with bright-painted doors that opened straight on to the pavements. Net curtains screened the interiors from view on most of them. There were a few people about, mainly women intent on doing their weekend shopping. Outside the post office a little black mongrel dog sat patiently waiting for its owner to emerge from inside. Ashley could not resist bending to pat it and it licked eagerly at her fingers. It would be nice to have a dog. She could never remember having a pet of any sort. She was sure Andrea liked dogs, too. Perhaps they could get one, so she could have a companion on her walks, because she intended to do lots of walking. She knew eventually she would have to look for a job and that this would probably entail travelling to Scarborough or some other town, but she wasn't going to think too much about that at the moment.

The street merged into a sort of steep cobbled causeway where there was a public house called The Galleon. The pub overlooked the harbour and next to it was a small shop whose doors stood open. It was the sort of shop that, judging from its crowded window, sold just about everything—toys, souvenirs, postcards, cheap jewellery. It was, in fact, called The Jewellery Box and Ashley first looked in the window and, seeing the notice 'You Are Welcome to Browse', went inside, having to bend her head to pass through the low doorway.

The inside was tiny and every available space was occupied. It was rather dark and Ashley did not at first see the woman behind the counter. She was sitting in a high-backed chair and when she said, 'Good-morning, love,' in a bright, chirpy voice Ashley jumped.

'Oh, good-morning,' she returned.

The woman was as small and quaint as her shop. A character right out of a story book. Grey hair in a neat bun; grey dress with a small white collar; steel-framed round glasses behind which her eyes positively twinkled.

'Does it rain?' the woman asked.

Ashley hesitated, not quite sure what the question meant, but the woman's accent was very broad Yorkshire so she presumed it was an enquiry as to the weather.

She smiled, 'Not so bad just at the moment.' She bent over the counter to study a tray of unusual silver rings.

'Pretty aren't they, love?' The little woman got out of her chair and leaned her arms on the counter.

'Very.' Ashley picked up a small ring with a black and white motif in the shape of two fishes. It would probably fit her little finger. She slipped it on to her right hand and it was a perfect fit. As the price was only £4.95 she said decisively, 'I'll take it,' glad that she had thought to put her purse in her pocket.

'Are you on holiday, love?' The woman busied herself at the old-fashioned cash register.

'No. I've come to live here. With my sister and brother-in-law. Mr and Mrs Winford.'

The woman's thin, friendly face broke into a bright smile. 'The new young vicar! Well, I never. A nice chap, what I've seen of him. 'Course I'm Chapel and not a regular attender at that so I'm not one of his flock, so to speak. Are you from the south, love?'

Ashley nodded. 'Yes. London.'

'Thought so. Could tell by your voice. Eh, lass, you'll find it a bit different living here in Storrs. P'r'aps you'll be bored.'

'Oh, I'm sure I shan't. Storrs seems a lovely place. Even in the rain.'

The woman folded her arms across her thin chest. 'Lovely in summer. Especially this year, but we can have some terrible winters. Not a lot of snow, p'r'aps, but gales. High seas, you know. I've lived here nigh on seventy years and I've known floods.' She shook her head sadly. 'Aye, loss of good lives sometimes 'n all.'

Ashley could tell the woman was prepared to chatter on for ever and, though she did not want to be rude, she did want to get on with her walk. She attempted as politely as she could to bring their conversation to an end.

'I expect I'll be seeing you again, Mrs ... ?' Her voice rose enquiringly.

'It's Miss, love. Miss France. Milly France and, yes, I expect our paths will cross some time or another, but I won't be behind this counter much longer. Retiring—well don't you think it's time I did at my age? Going to sell up when my solicitor gets a move on, that is.'

'Oh, dear, will that mean you'll be leaving Storrs, Miss France?' Ashley asked, moving discreetly a bit nearer the door.

'Milly. Everybody calls me Milly. I know

everybody and everybody knows me. Oh, no, shan't be leaving here, love. Born and bred in Storrs. Where else would I go? No, I'll still have me little cottage, next to the post office it is, but I'm selling the shop. Lock, stock and barrel.'

'By the way, my name's Ashley. Ashley Elliott.' Ashley tried another tack, changing the subject, with her hand on the door knob.

'Eh, unusual name Ashley! What's happened to the good, old-fashioned Mauds and Marys, that's what I'd like to know!' She chuckled with delight and Ashley finally left the little shop and the little woman with a light step, feeling all the better for having met Miss Milly France.

As if to match her mood the rain had now stopped and a weak sun was breaking through the clouds. Ashley folded up her umbrella and tucked it under her arm. She walked away from The Jewellery Box and further out along the cobbled causeway that ran beside the harbour wall. The tide was out, white-foamed breakers in the distance and boats, motor-boats, sailing boats, some big, some small were dry-dock moored. The wind seemed to have dropped along with the last of the rain and the sea was quite calm, but Ashley could see that this was a rugged stretch of coastline, where the sea birds screeched and wheeled continually along the cliffsides. Further out along the causeway the harbour gave way to a stretch of pebbly beach reached by wooden steps.

The tide was well out and Ashley felt it would be quite safe to walk along the beach. Perhaps she could make for the grassy headland in the distance that jutted out and joined a sort of rocky bank. From where she was, Ashley could not see beyond this headland. It may be there was another beach out of her vision.

She went down the wooden steps and started walking along the beach parallel to the causeway, which she now saw seemed to stretch for quite some distance. There were more houses along the far side of this causeway, and even a handful of guesthouses with names like Sea View and Bella Vista. In summer no doubt Storrs was thriving. It would never be a Scarborough or a Whitby but must, Ashley felt sure, attract its quota of visitors who preferred a quiet, unspoilt holiday venue, or who liked to sail or fish.

Little Milly France's shop must really come into its own in the season. Ashley glanced at her finger with its new silver ring. It was unusual. It suddenly occurred to her that The Jewellery Box had not been the usual run-of-the-mill seaside souvenir shop but more of a curio shop. Quaint and fascinating. Now it was to be up for sale.

'Fancy running a shop, Ashley?' she asked herself out loud. The idea was idiotic and she laughed and started to run along the beach, her feet skittering the pebbles and crushing the various discarded shells. The wind blew her hair back from her face. It felt good. Her speed increased.

She could not remember ever running like this before since she was a child.

Then, suddenly she realized she had almost reached the outcrop of dark rocks and she slowed down her speed, a little out of breath now. When she got to the rocks it was easy to scramble up them and over the other side. It was worth the effort. She found herself gazing at more jagged cliffs with another wide curve of pebbly beach, but incredibly the tide seemed much closer at this point and was definitely coming in fast. No matter. She could quickly turn the way she had come, but it was rather foolish of her to come so far along the beach without checking on the tides.

She turned to scramble back down the rocks and got another shock. How stupid of her! Of course the sea this side of the rocks must be keeping some sort of pace with the sea on the other side. She looked towards the village centre, seeing the square tower of St Mark's church rising plainly above the rest of the buildings.

How far away Storrs looked. Had she really run so far?

She started back across the beach but did not get very far. The waves, only small it was true, but still enough to wet her feet were beginning to lap around her. Should she keep on back to the village or climb up the rocks again?

She was beginning to feel really frightened by now and knew she would have to come to a quick decision: go on towards Storrs, literally racing the tide, or go back to the safety of the rocks. But would she be safe there? They weren't, upon reflection, all that high and she could not possibly scramble up the side of the headland itself.

The sea was round her ankles now, the brownish foam breaking up around her, receding then advancing, leaving a trail of small glistening pebbles. Quickly Ashley turned and splashed back towards the rocks. The base of the rocks was wet and slippery, where only moments before it had merely been damp from the rainfall. As she tried to scramble out of the sea's way her feet kept slipping and sliding. The waves were spuming upwards against the rocks, showering her, and the hem of her trench coat was drenched.

She stumbled and put out her hands to grasp the rock above her. The sea washed over her grasping fingers. It was icy cold.

Oh God! Ashley was praying silently now. She wasn't going to be safe. Not here. She would have to climb higher. She would have to try for the face of the craggy headland. It was her only chance. Not looking backwards, telling herself the sea wasn't pounding and advancing so close behind her she managed to make her way to the other end of the outcrop of rocks. The face of the headland did not look so bad now she was closer to it. If she could get a good foot- and finger-hold. If she could maintain her grasp. If she could pull herself up. Please, God, help me, she prayed.

She was beginning to think she would make it, even though her arms ached and her chest was straining with the effort of climbing and of concentration, when her right foot missed the foothold she was fumbling for and she jarred her right shin on a piece of jagged rock. She let out a loud yelp of pain and for a fraction of a second, without thinking, she loosened her fingers' hold on the rock. God, she was going to fall. She was going backwards. Her hands flailed the empty air and her body fell away from the face of the headland. She landed on the rocks below with an almighty thud, hitting the side of her head, blacking out immediately.

Four

Ashley opened her eyes. She was lying down on a very narrow, hard bed with a rough blanket thrown over her. There was a throbbing pain in her left temple and everything seemed to be moving; floating—no, that wasn't the right word, but she could not think of the right one to describe the sensation. A gentle bobbing movement.

It came to her with a rush. The sea! The rocks! Her fall! Instinctively she touched her temple, feeling the piece of sticking plaster, wincing with the sudden pain as she realized she was on a boat. Of course. That was it. A boat.

She sat up, hitting her head; giving a loud yell at the injustice of hurting her already painful head. She was on the

57

bottom bunk of a two-tier pair, in a small, narrow cabin. On the opposite wall was a long counter painted grey which contained a masculine-looking brush and comb and a half-full bottle of aftershave set neatly before a free-standing square mirror in a brown plastic frame. Above the counter was a port-hole. Ignoring the pain in her head, Ashley climbed off the bunk. She must look out of that port-hole. If she was out at sea, where were they heading? Had she been rescued off the rocks by someone only to be kidnapped by whoever it was?

It wasn't until she had satisfied herself that the boat was, in fact, safely moored in the harbour, among the other boats, bobbing and lilting now on the high tide, that Ashley discovered she was no longer wearing her jeans and that her sweater ended ridiculously above her pair of white bikini pants, leaving the rest of her, legs and feet, bare. She picked up the blanket and wrapped it round her.

Who had removed her jeans, her shoes

and socks? Who did the boat belong to? There was only one way to find out. Bare-legged or no bare-legged, she would have to leave this cabin. Even as she thought this the door opened and a man stood in the doorway. A tall, dark-haired man of about thirty. He was wearing dark trousers, tucked into huge wellington boots and a thick, polo-necked navy blue sweater. A black sailor-type peaked cap was pushed well back on his dark curly hair. His face was very brown, weather-beaten, and he had dark, almost black eyes. Ashley took in her rescuer's appearance in the few brief moments before he came further into the cabin and said, 'So you're awake. Welcome back. I thought I was going to have to fetch Doc Branson.'

His voice was curt, and though he used the word 'welcome' there was no such meaning evident.

'Where are my clothes?' Ashley demanded in a voice which came out sharper than she had intended.

The man rested his hand casually against the doorframe. 'Drying by the stove. Probably dry by now,' he said.

'Then may I please have them back?' She clutched the blanket around her, feeling, and she was certain, looking ridiculous.

'I didn't hear you say "thank you".' The man did not move.

For some reason Ashley felt angry with him. He had probably saved her life, but there was something about his attitude that irritated her. He hadn't smiled once. She did not yet know how he had come to find her on the rocks but it wasn't difficult to grasp that he had probably been at sea and had seen her lying there. She was grateful, of course she was, but for the life of her she could not find the words to tell him so.

'Why didn't you take me straight to a doctor?' she threw at him. 'I was unconscious, wasn't I? How did you know I wasn't seriously hurt? Did you have to keep me on board your boat?'

'You were soaking wet.' A lazy smile

touched his mouth for only a brief moment. 'At least the bottom half of you was. I thought it best to bring you into harbour and get you dried out. As for being hurt, a small piece of sticking-plaster took care of that. And you were damned lucky, young woman. What on earth made you head for those rocks when the tide was coming in?'

She lifted her head defiantly at his words. 'How do you know I did?'

'Know?' His eyebrows rose. 'You were lowered on to there by helicopter I suppose.'

Ashley flushed. He was enjoying this and whoever he was she did not have to put up with his arrogance.

'Please fetch my clothes, and I'll get out of here,' she said.

'I'll fetch your clothes but you're not leaving till you have some hot soup. I wouldn't like to think I'd saved your life just to have you die of pneumonia.'

He was right. He had saved her life.

For the first time since finding herself here Ashley realized what a lucky escape she had had. Her legs went suddenly weak and she was forced to sit down on the edge of the lower bunk. She put her hands over her face, half expecting the man to come further into the cabin to see if she was all right, perhaps, but when she looked up he had gone. He wasn't away long, returning with her jeans, socks and shoes tucked under his arm whilst he carried in his hands a wooden tray bearing a bowl of steaming soup, which smelt divine, and a chunk of crusty bread.

'Now be a good girl and eat it all up. Then I'll take you home.'

He set the tray on the counter under the porthole. Ashley decided to call a truce. She realized she was very hungry and wondered what time it was. She glanced at her watch, which thankfully seemed to have survived her ordeal unscathed. Goodness, it was after one o'clock. Andrea would be worried about her.

'I'm sorry if I sounded ungrateful.' She still kept the grey blanket across her knees. No way was she going to get dressed whilst he was there. 'But I was a bit startled to find myself on a boat.'

There came the brief, sardonic smile again. 'Thought perhaps you'd fallen into the hands of a white-slaver, did you?' he asked.

'No, of course not. It was just a shock, that's all. I *was* knocked out, you know.'

'I know. Does your head hurt? Would you like an aspirin?'

Did his voice sound sympathetic? Ashley glanced up sharply but the man's expression was bland. If he felt any concern for her it did not show on his face.

'No thank you. I'm all right.'

'Your soup's getting cold,' he nodded towards the tray. 'I'll be back.' By the door he hesitated. 'By the way, the head's just opposite.'

'The what?' she asked.

'The head. The loo. The toilet. The lavatory.'

Ashley felt her face redden. She could have kicked herself for being so ignorant. She was sure she heard the man chuckle as he left the cabin. What an unpleasant person he was! Perhaps he had expected her to grovel at his feet because he had rescued her. If so he was doomed to disappointment. She had told him she was grateful. Surely that was enough.

As soon as she was alone she scrambled into her jeans and then attacked the bowl of vegetable soup. It tasted so good; out of a can no doubt, but thick and savoury. The bread was soft on the inside, crusty on the outside and it did not take Ashley long to finish both bread and soup. She went and opened the cabin door. The passage outside was deserted. Quickly she scampered across to the door on the other side. The toilet cubicle—sorry, 'the head'—was small and spotlessly clean with a white washbasin, soap and a neatly folded clean towel. If the man lived aboard his boat he seemed to have everything shipshape and Bristol fashion. It wasn't such a small boat either. There were two doors on the same side as the cabin and one more on the other side. At the far end steps led upwards. Ashley went to them and emerged on to the deck. The rain had ceased completely and the clouds were breaking up.

The harbour was busy with boats but there seemed to be a shortage of people. Overhead the seagulls swooped and dived making a lot of noise. Ashley glanced around the boat. She knew nothing at all about boats of any description but could see this one was well fitted-out, gleaming and clean with blue and white paintwork and dark-polished floors. It did not appear to have a sail so there must be a motor somewhere, or rather an engine, she tried to think nautically. At the moment the wheelhouse was deserted so where was her rescuer?

Ashley remembered a sea-trip three years ago, before the advent of Karl, when she had gone to Yugoslavia with a girlfriend. They had gone by local bus from Cavtat to Dubrovnik and returned by boat. This boat was a similar type and size. Was it then a pleasure-craft used perhaps for ferrying holidaymakers around? It was then she saw the blue-and-white painted notice fastened to the side of the wheelhouse:

'Brad Thornton, Sea Trips. Fishing Trips. By the Hour. By the Day. By the Week.' There was also a telephone number but it did not register with Ashley. So that was his name. Brad Thornton. And where was he now? She could not see him anywhere.

Perhaps she could leave now, by herself. There was a gangplank down to the quay. A couple of minutes and she could be away, before Brad Thornton re-appeared from wherever he had hidden himself. Andrea would be really worried by now. And any midday meal she may have prepared would be ruined.

She moved quickly towards the gang-plank, but had not set one foot on it when she heard him speaking close behind her. He must be as soft-footed as a cat!

'Don't you want this?'

Ashley swung round. Brad Thornton was holding out her raincoat. She had completely forgotten its existence. She took it from him, mumbling her thanks. Then she remembered Andrea's umbrella but that, no doubt, had been washed away with the tide by now.

'And now I'll take you home, wherever that may be,' he said.

'It's all right,' Ashley returned. 'I can find my own way, thank you.'

'I consider it my duty and it isn't open to argument.' If only he would smile. He had quite a nice face. In fact, he was rather good-looking in a rugged outdoor sort of way. But he looked at her as though she were nothing. Well, the feeling was mutual. He probably thought she was a miserable so-and-so as well. It didn't matter a jot. Storrs may only be a small village but Ashley was going to do her utmost to make certain that their paths did not cross again. As she had no intention of taking a fishing-trip and Brad Thornton did not look like a regular church-goer, it should not be too difficult.

He gave a mocking little bow. 'After you, Miss ... er?'

'My name's Ashley Elliott.' If you must know, she added to herself.

'And I'm ...'

Rudely Ashley interrupted, 'Yes I know. I can read.'

She started to walk down the gangplank, knowing that he was following on close behind. There was nothing for it but to let Mr Brad Thornton take her back to the vicarage. What sort of a name was Brad anyway? It must be short for something else. Bradley? Bradford? Who knew? Who cared?

'Here's the old jalopy.' As they reached

the quayside, Brad Thornton moved ahead of her to where a dark blue Volvo estate car was parked. As it had the current year's registration letter, he must have been attempting a feeble joke. She did not answer, but turned to him and told him again that she was perfectly able to make her own way home.

He did not even bother to speak, opening the Volvo's passenger's door then going round to the driver's side. With a sigh Ashley got into the car. It was as smart inside as out but travelling in expensive motor cars was not exactly a new experience for her. She did not own a car herself—she could not even drive—but Karl owned a Triumph Stag and a Granada Ghia and she had been in both. Thinking of Karl now for the first time in ages made Ashley realize what a great contrast there was between him and the man now sitting beside her. He had his hands on the steering-wheel. They were large; calloused. Karl had fine, well-kept hands and would not have been seen dead in those awful trousers.

'Where to?' his voice broke in on her thoughts.

'Do you know St Mark's vicarage?'

Slowly his head turned towards her. He had an expression on his face which Ashley could only describe as contemptuous.

'Don't tell me you're the new vicar's wife?' he asked.

'No, I'm not, but I'm his wife's sister.'

A thin smile crossed his mouth. 'So that explains your attitude.'

'What attitude? What do you mean?' Annoyance at him was rising in her again.

Brad Thornton started up the car. The engine purred gently. Of course!

'Your arrogant attitude, as though you were doing me a favour by allowing me to snatch you off those rocks. Typical!'

It didn't help to cool Ashley's temper by knowing that her attitude had been, if not exactly arrogant then far short of grateful to him.

'Am I to be beholden to you for the rest of my life for God's sake?' she cried.

Immediately she knew she had played right into his hands by blaspheming and could cheerfully have cut her tongue out.

'Oh, naughty girl!' he scoffed. 'You'd better say three Hail Marys and a Glory Be ...'

Coldly she stared him out. 'I'm an Anglican, not a Roman Catholic,' she told him.

'You're all the same,' Brad Thornton's voice was bitter.

It was obvious that for some reason known only to himself he had a grudge against the Church. He had been bad enough towards her before she had told him she was the local vicar's sister-in-law. Now he was being sarcastic and sneering.

Taking a deep breath Ashley resolved to say no more. She would refuse to let him rile her.

He seemed to have little or no regard for his new car as he drove it like a madman through the village. He did not bother to put on his seat-belt and Ashley half-hoped a policeman would see him flouting the law, but did not really believe one would. If there was a local policeman about somewhere he would probably be well known to the owner of a local fishing-boat. They might even be great friends, in a 'you scratch my back, I'll scratch your back' sort of way.

It did not take long to reach the vicarage and neither of them spoke another word during the journey. Brad drew the Volvo to a screeching halt outside the gates. Apparently he did not intend to take her right to the door. Ashley was glad. It removed the obligation to invite him inside. If Peter was at home she knew Brad Thornton would be made most welcome. Peter was not the sort of person who could be unpleasant to anybody. She could well imagine that Brad Thornton would take great delight in trying to make mincemeat of the young vicar.

'Thank you for the lift,' she said politely. 'And for everything else.'

'For saving your life you mean. Why can't you bring yourself to admit it, Miss Elliott?'

'And why must you always crow about it?' Quickly Ashley opened the car door and climbed out, closing it firmly behind her. She didn't look back as she walked up the drive, but she heard him start up and drive away.

As she reached the house the front door opened and Andrea stood there, a look of relief on her face, but Ashley could see her sister had been worrying. Suddenly there was a lump in her throat and she started to cry as the awful remembrance of the morning's events swept over her.

'Oh, Andrea!' She fell sobbing into her startled sister's arms.

Five

Peter was out. Though reluctant to leave his wife alone when she was worried about Ashley, he had an appointment to meet a group of schoolchildren from Whitby, who were coming with their history teacher to do some brass rubbings in the church. So Ashley found herself being cosseted by Andrea and later, having expressed curiosity about the church and its history, she listened whilst Andrea told her as much about St Mark's fifteenth century church as she knew. Information about Mr Brad Thornton was not so easily come by.

When Ashley had told her own story about the morning's happenings, Andrea had given her a warm hug and taken her to the warm-smelling kitchen where she and Peter had recently eaten their lunch. Andrea even apologized that they had not waited for Ashley to come home, but Ashley would not hear of it.

'I'm the one who should apologize to you,' she said and felt even worse when she had to decline the quiche and salad which Andrea was hastening to produce. She explained about the soup and bread which had been so filling and satisfying.

Andrea said, 'You'll have a cup of coffee though, won't you?' And they sat by the big kitchen table to drink it.

By then Ashley was feeling much better.

'I know he thought I was a spoiled brat,' she said, 'but there was something about him. Oh, I can't say what. I've never been so irritated in my life before by a person I've only just met, and who has probably just saved my life.'

'Do you think you imagined his surliness?' Andrea asked charitably. 'I mean, perhaps you were feeling a little bit guilty, about going on to the rocks. Perhaps you had your back up, if you see what I mean.'

This was so near the truth that Ashley was about to snap Andrea's head off. She swallowed hard.

'Yes, I suppose you're right,' she said. 'It was a stupid thing to do, not checking on the tide. And I did feel a fool, I must admit, besides being frightened. Do you think I should go back to Mr Thornton's boat and tell him I'm sorry?'

Andrea smiled. 'If he's there you could, I suppose.'

'And if he isn't?' Ashley did not at all relish confronting Brad Thornton again, but decided she would give him the benefit of the doubt. If she went, prepared to eat humble pie and he accepted the apology and was pleasant about it, it would mean Andrea was right and perhaps she and Brad Thornton could set off on the right foot the second time!

'I must admit,' Andrea was saying, 'that I don't know who he is so I can't give you any pointers as to where he might live. He doesn't come to St Mark's and I'm afraid at the moment Peter and I are still feeling our feet as far as our parishioners are concerned. We hope, of course, to be able to get to know everyone in Storrs eventually, whether they belong to St Marks or not, but obviously that's going to take time.'

Believing there was no time like the present, Ashley resolved to walk down to the harbour on Saturday morning to see if she could find Mr Thornton. It was another grey drizzly but not too cold day and after helping with the Saturday chores she left the vicarage. Andrea had given her a short shopping list to pick up from the butcher's and the greengrocer's, reminding her that they both closed at noon. Ashley laughed. 'Don't worry, I shan't go anywhere near the beach,' she promised.

In the afternoon they were going to drive into Scarborough so Ashley could have a look around. Peter wouldn't need the van as he was meeting a young couple at the church to go through their forthcoming wedding.

As she walked down the drive Ashley realized she had not yet seen inside the church. Now was as good a time as any. She knew the church would be open. Peter unlocked the main doors every morning and did not re-lock them till dusk. Coming from London, Ashley had expressed concern at the advisability of this, but when Peter had said seriously, 'It's God's House. Someone might need to go in there. Who am I to stop them?' she could not argue. Now she was glad and as she entered the quiet vestibule and pulled open the inner door, she knew instinctively that Peter was right. At the moment the church was deserted and Ashley was very conscious of her own quiet footsteps as she walked slowly down the central aisle.

It was a beautiful church; only small, and surprisingly light inside despite the greyness of the morning. Above the altar was an exquisite stained-glass window depicting the same scene as the picture in her bedroom. *The Light of the World.* Reds, blues, greens. If ever the sun shone through this window the effect must be magnificent. Around the white-painted walls and stone pillars were carved wooden plaques denoting the Stations of the Cross, rather unusual she thought in a non-Catholic church. A plain silver cross and candlesticks stood on the covered altar table and the pulpit was most beautifully and intricately carved with a ruby-red and gold drop-cloth. Flowers stood in small vases on the side altar.

A small, simple, peaceful church and Ashley found herself sitting down for a moment or two silently being grateful for her escape from the sea the previous day.

When she came out of the church she breathed in the fresh sea air and set off at a brisk pace towards the centre of the village. She felt she was now in the right frame of mind to meet Brad Thornton and hoped he would be aboard his boat, but when she reached the harbour, neither Brad nor his boat were to be seen. There were mooring ropes and a painted notice on a sort of wooden stand which told her much the same as the notice on the boat had done. Evidently Brad Thornton was at sea. He must have gone out on an earlier tide because the high tide of yesterday had not yet appeared in the dry harbour. Ashley did not see any point in hanging around. The boat may not return for hours. She turned and walked back up to the main street, a bit disappointed that her feeling of being 'all right with the world' was to be wasted.

She did Andrea's shopping, finding both shop assistants and fellow customers friendly and pleasant. Everyone she met had a quite open and frank curiosity about her and in a few brief moments she had told them she was the new vicar's sister-in-law. Words of praise for Peter and Andrea came swiftly and it was obvious that during their short time in Storrs her sister and brother-in-law had created a good impression.

She was passing the post office when the blue-painted door of the adjoining cottage opened and Milly France came out.

'Why it's Ashley, isn't it?' The little, bird-like woman beamed, closing her front door and locking it carefully with a stout key.

'Yes. How are you this morning, Milly?'

'Very well, thank you. Just going down to the shop. I don't open very long hours in winter. You don't get the visitors then, you see. Summertime, it's another story.'

'Have you found a buyer for your shop yet?' Ashley asked.

'Not yet, no, but I've got the notice up now. Have you seen it?'

Ashley had to admit that she hadn't. She had been too busy thinking about what she was going to say to Brad Thornton to notice Milly's shop at all.

Milly went on, keeping Ashley talking

on the doorstep. 'Mind you, I've been having second thoughts since I spoke to you last.'

'What about?'

'About selling up. I thought I might just sell the stock at valuation and the goodwill, of course, but simply rent the shop premises. Don't you think that's a good idea, Ashley? It's in a good position and property values being what they are. I have a little washroom at the back, you know, and a kitchenette affair. A little gold mine in summer.'

Ashley was sure it must be, and the thought stirred in her mind again that she might like to try her hand at running a little shop. Milly France's was ideal and even more so now there would only be rent to pay.

'Come and have tea with me tomorrow, will you?' Milly surprised her by saying. 'I expect you'll be busy Sunday morning. Church and all. Then your traditional Sunday dinner. Roast beef and Yorkshire pudding. Mustn't miss that.'

Ashley did not know what sort of midday meal Andrea would produce on Sunday, but judging from her sister's cooking so far it would certainly be something to look forward to.

'I'd love to come to tea,' she said.

It occurred to her that Milly might know something about Brad Thornton. Possibly she would be the ideal person to quiz about him.

She returned happily to the vicarage, despite the sudden heavy downpour of rain that gave every indication of setting in for the day. Peter was emerging from his study. He was wearing his black cassock, no doubt because of his afternoon appointment with the engaged couple.

'Raining again?' he grinned.

'Haven't you noticed? It's teeming down.' Ashley removed her coat and gave it a shake.

'I never notice anything when I'm writing my sermon,' Peter said. 'The house could burn down around me and I wouldn't even smell it.'

Ashley laughed. 'I sincerely hope not,' she said.

He followed her into the kitchen. It seemed to be the favourite room in the house and it was comfortable and friendly with the warmth from the solid fuel cooker; the big, old-fashioned table around which to sit with a mug of milky coffee; the cheerful primrose-yellow of the cupboards and formica work-tops.

Andrea as usual was busy, this time with washing up what looked like the aftermath of a morning's baking session and indeed the evidence of such a morning was present in the appetizing aroma drifting round the kitchen and the tantalizing mounds on cooling trays hidden under clean tea-cloths.

Ashley picked up a spare tea-cloth to go and dry up, whilst Peter went to have a stealthy peep under one of the cloths on the table.

'Mmm ... scones!' he breathed.

'And not to be pilfered by you!' Andrea warned him, but Ashley knew she was only pretending and Peter didn't seem to care one way or the other, blithely removing a still-warm scone and disappearing from the kitchen with it.

Ashley said, 'Shopping accomplished without a hitch.'

Andrea turned to smile at her. 'Good. Put the kettle on, love, let's have a coffee.'

Ashley hastened to do so. 'And a scone?' she said.

'Or a piece of apple pie.'

'Oh, goody!' Home-made cakes and pies were unknown to Ashley. But this kitchen cried out for them. I shall learn to bake, Ashley promised herself.

'I've been invited out to tea,' she told Andrea as she returned to finish the drying up.

'Not with Mr Thornton?' Andrea's eyes had an excited gleam.

Ashley laughed. 'Oh, no fear. I didn't

even see him. His boat wasn't there. But I saw Milly France coming out of her house. We met briefly yesterday when I went into her shop. Do you know her?'

'Of course. Everybody knows Milly. She's a Methodist I think, we don't see her at St Mark's anyway.'

'She did say she was "chapel" whatever that means. Anyway, she asked me to have tea with her. I'm going tomorrow about four. Is that all right?'

'Of course it is. You can do what you like.' Andrea pulled out the plug. 'She's a nice person, isn't she? She's been running that little shop of hers since she was a girl apparently. Knows all there is to know about Storrs. Hey, I should imagine she knows where your Mr Thornton lives.'

'He's not *my* Mr Thornton,' Ashley pronounced stoutly. 'But I expect you're right about Milly knowing his whereabouts. I've got a feeling he's a local, too. He certainly looked as though he knew a thing or two about boats and as though he spent most of his time outdoors.'

'Good-looking, was he?' Andrea gave her sister a sidelong glance.

'Not particularly. Not my type anyway. I'm used to the City type of man.'

'Like your Karl for instance?'

Ashley nodded. 'Exactly.'

Now why had she deliberately led her sister to believe she preferred men in smart suits, ties and with neat, well-groomed hair and nails? It was true Karl was like that but how many other men friends had she had for goodness' sake? Karl was certainly the only one she had been serious about.

From her brief glimpses of men in Storrs there did not seem an over-abundance of any type, let alone of her own age. Well, that suited her fine. She had no intention of getting involved with any man. She was enjoying being carefree and the prospects of an uncluttered future without entanglements was one she relished.

On Sunday afternoon when Ashley arrived

at Milly France's cottage she was welcomed into the warm, cosy sitting-room. The door was so low she had to bend to enter and she was only 5′ 4″. She could well imagine Karl cursing if he had to come into this room. Not to mention Brad Thornton. He would positively dwarf it!

There was a fire burning cheerfully in the old-fashioned fireplace. A most welcome sight because even though it wasn't very cold, the damp and wetness outside made it seem so. Milly's home was as neat and tiny as herself. A ponderously ticking clock stood on the mantelpiece. Chairs were covered in flowered cretonne with plump matching cushions. Frilly white curtains maintained the privacy of the room from passers-by on the street outside. There was a crowded china cabinet, a small, lace-covered table with plants in green pots and when Milly had brought in the tea on a wooden tray she followed up with a three-tier wooden cake-stand of a type Ashley had only seen in antique shop windows. Milly was wearing another dove-grey dress with white collar and cuffs, giving her a Quaker-like appearance. She was a quick-moving little woman and obviously eager to please.

'And how are you settling in Storrs, Ashley?' she asked, pouring out tea from a round brown pot.

'I think I shall like living here,' Ashley replied. 'Everyone seems so nice and friendly.'

Milly's eyes twinkled behind their glasses. 'Well, we try to be.' She pointed to the cake-stand. 'Help yourself to a sandwich or a cake.'

Each tier of the stand held a doily covered plate. One contained small brown-bread sandwiches, one buttered scones and the third a variety of small iced cakes in paper cases. Far too much for two people, especially only a couple of hours after consuming a huge Sunday lunch, but Ashley did not want to offend Milly and she balanced a plate on her knee and took a sandwich. It was salmon and cucumber and tasted delicious.

'I've been thinking about your shop, Milly,' she said when she had emptied her mouth. 'You said you had decided to rent it out. Would you be prepared to let me rent it?'

Milly looked surprised. 'You?' she cried.

Ashley nodded. 'Yes. I gave up my job to come here to live with Andrea, my sister, and her husband.'

'Oh, I see. You were in a similar line of business in London, were you?'

'No,' Ashley admitted with a smile. 'I worked in a bank. To be honest I hadn't really thought about taking another job just yet, but my father died recently and left me some money and your shop's so quaint and exciting. Of course, I wouldn't want to buy it, I couldn't really afford to do that, but you said something about selling the stock and renting the building and I'm sure we could come to some arrangement.' She took a drink of her tea. 'Would you consider me, please?'

Milly looked absolutely delighted. 'Nothing would please me more. A young person is just what the shop needs. And I'd feel happy knowing you were in charge.'

'That's nice of you to say so.' Ashley knew she and Miss Milly France were going to be great friends, despite the difference in their ages.

Whilst they ate, Milly insisted on discussing business details, promising to contact her solicitor first thing in the morning. There was no time like the present, she said. As she talked and Ashley was quite content to listen, inevitably she began to talk about Storrs, her voice full of love and pride for her home village, for her friends and neighbours.

Suddenly, before she could change her mind, Ashley said, 'I expect you know Mr Brad Thornton.'

'Brad Thornton? Now which Brad Thornton do you mean? The old one or the young one?'

So there were two of them. Father and son no doubt.

'I guess he'll be the younger one,' Ashley said. 'He has a boat in the harbour. For fishing trips.'

Milly nodded knowingly, brushing a few crumbs off her skirt. 'Ah, yes. That's young Bradley Thornton. Bradley Senior is dead now. Has been for some five years.' She sounded sad. 'Oh, it's a sad story. What happened to the Thorntons, I mean.'

Ashley was all ears. 'What did happen to them?' Her voice was eager. She had a feeling Milly would be more than willing to impart any knowledge she possessed. She was not disappointed.

'Well,' the little woman settled herself in the deep armchair that seemed much too big for her, 'they own the big house on Troon Island. In fact they own the whole island. Perhaps you haven't heard of it yet?'

'No, I haven't,' Ashley admitted, hoping

Milly wasn't going to digress.

'It's an island and it isn't, if you know what I mean. There's a sort of causeway leading from the beach about two miles north of Storrs. When there's a high tide you can't get either one way or the other, except by boat, of course.'

And that wouldn't worry Brad Thornton, Ashley thought.

Milly went on. 'When Bradley Senior was a young man, there were plenty of comings and goings across that causeway, I can tell you. Parties and gatherings.' She took on a wistful look.

'Did you go?' Ashley asked.

'Oh, yes. Sometimes guests stayed the night. There were plenty of rooms in the Manor House. Young Bradley was just a little boy then. A real little gentleman he was.'

Ashley was about to remark, 'How he's changed!' but thought better of it.

'Then Bradley Senior's wife died. Young Brad's mother. A lovely woman. Bradley was devastated. Inconsolable. I'm sorry to say that the parties came to an end and Bradley became almost a recluse. The saddest thing was that he seemed to turn against the boy, who incidentally was the spitting image of his mother. He sent the lad away to boarding-school.' Milly shuddered as though the memory upset her. 'He came back occasionally for holidays, but his father spent as little time with him as possible. They became like two strangers and when young Bradley was about eighteen, he left Troon Island and Storrs for good. No one ever knew where he went. Bradley Senior never ventured to tell his son's whereabouts so that was that.'

'But he's back here now,' Ashley said.

'Oh, yes, he came back five years ago when the old man died. Well, stands to reason, doesn't it, the island and the Manor House were his by rights then. He lives out there now, but he doesn't welcome visitors. If you were to meet him in the village he would be polite and civil, pass the time of day with you he would, but that's as far as it goes. Soon after he came back here there were various rumours circulating about him, you know how village people are. Nobody can keep a secret no matter how they try. I remember once when I ...'

Quickly Ashley broke in, 'What sort of rumours?'

'Well, that young Bradley had suffered some terrible tragedy. I don't mean the death of his father, I don't suppose he cared one way or another about that, but he left here little more than a boy and he returned a man, but he's never tried to ... well ... to fit in here and nobody's ever been invited to Troon Island. They do say,' here she leaned forward confidentially, 'that the old Manor House has gone to wrack and ruin. First the old man stopped caring about it and then when he died, young Bradley came back and settled for living in a cottage in the grounds. Of course, it's all hearsay and probably to be taken with a pinch of salt, but local fishermen who pass by Troon Island have told tales. Bradley's doing well with his own fishing-boat, I believe, but in between times he seems to vanish off the face of the earth.'

What Milly was saying seemed to fit in so well with what Ashley knew about Brad Thornton. She was debating whether to tell her new friend that she had already met 'young Bradley' when Milly forestalled her.

'And how do you know there's such a person as Brad Thornton anyway? Surely you haven't been listening to local gossip already.'

Ashley smiled to herself. Dear little Milly was blithely unaware that Ashley need listen to no one but her to hear all the gossip she needed. She decided to be completely honest and related the incident of yesterday. Milly was full of sympathy. 'Oh, dear, you were fortunate! Those tides can be treacherous. It's a very rugged coastline. Causes all sorts of unpredictable currents.'

When Milly asked Ashley if she was interested in lace-making and took her on a tour of the cottage to let her see some of her own handiwork, Ashley realized that for the time being at least the subject of Brad Thornton was over. Soon after, she left the cottage, promising to keep in touch about the business of the shop, and hurried back to the vicarage to get ready for evensong, but throughout the service her concentration was poor. She could not get Brad Thornton out of her mind. If it was true that he had suffered some personal tragedy perhaps that would account for his surliness and unpleasantness. Ashley was relieved to know that she could not be blamed for Brad's attitude if the whole of Storrs found him an awkward customer! Nevertheless, she had a certain amount of sympathy for him. He must have had a pretty rotten time of it after his mother died, being sent away from a place he must have loved dearly. Now he was back and had been living on Troon Island for five years, but not, according to Milly, in the main Manor House.

'I should like to visit Troon Island,' Ashley found herself thinking; then quickly brought her thoughts back to the present when she realized that out of the whole congregation she was the only person still kneeling.

Six

'By the way,' Ashley announced at breakfast on Monday morning, 'I'm thinking of going into business.'

Peter looked up from his boiled egg. Andrea was only having tea and lightly done toast. She had woken up that day feeling a bit queazy. She had imagined that her bouts of morning sickness, which had never been severe, were over and done with, so her upset stomach was all the more surprising. However, she had insisted on coming downstairs and waved aside any suggestions that she should be mollycoddled.

The more Ashley saw of her sister the more she had to admire her. She was involved in so much Church work as well as being a housewife. Perhaps the rambling old vicarage was a bit on the untidy side, but Andrea gained top marks in Ashley's book for her cooking and baking and that meant more than a high gloss on a polished table would have done.

She was also an accomplished knitter and clever with a needle, compiling an ever-growing pile of baby garments and little woollies. Ashley was convinced that when talents were allotted she had been missed out altogether.

Now she felt pleased that she was announcing something concerning herself. Her sister and brother-in-law certainly looked surprised.

'Business?' Peter repeated. 'What kind of business?'

'I'm thinking of taking over Milly France's shop.'

There was a slight pause then Andrea cried, 'Why, that's wonderful.'

Ashley grimaced. 'I'm sure what you'd really like to say is "What do you know about running a shop?"'

'No, really,' Andrea demurred, 'but what brought the idea about?'

Ashley explained about Milly's original intention to sell her shop and that she had now changed her mind and decided to rent it.

'And that's where I come in.' Ashley concluded. 'Don't you think it's a good idea?'

'I think it's a great idea!' Andrea smiled. 'But do you think you'll have enough money with what Dad left you? You can always have some of mine. Can't she, Peter?'

'If you want her to, then yes, by all means.' Equable, easy-going Peter was more than willing to agree, but Ashley would not hear of it.

'I can manage,' she told them. 'I'm really quite excited about the whole prospect. Something entirely different from what I've been used to.'

'A change is as good as a rest,' Peter said with a grin.

'You'll have to ask Miss France to come and have a meal with us some time,' Andrea said.

'Even if she is "chapel",' Peter's face was solemn but his eyes were not.

Andrea gave him a little shake and they both laughed. Once again Ashley was acutely aware of the chemistry that existed between Andrea and Peter. She was sure it was a rare and precious gift and not for the first time she felt twinges of envy.

When Andrea said, 'Did Milly know anything about Brad Thornton?' Ashley's first instinct was to rush in with the story Milly had told her, but something made her hold back. There was no earthly reason why her sister and brother-in-law should not know but all she said was, 'She knew something about him, yes. He is a local man, though he's been living away for a good few years. I think I shall wait till I see his boat in the harbour before trying to say "thank you".'

They accepted this but Ashley did not feel comfortable because she had not really been honest with them. She fully intended at least going to look at Troon Island, so why couldn't she have said so?

Immediately she knew the answer. She did not want Andrea to look at her with that sort of sisterly, knowing look she had had before when Brad's name was mentioned. She did not want Andrea, or Peter either, to start having ideas and notions that were way, way off the mark. Once more Ashley reiterated with herself that there wasn't a man on God's green earth in whom she had the slightest interest.

Because Andrea wasn't feeling too good Ashley postponed her visit to Troon Island, if 'visit' it could be called. She wouldn't go across there! All the same when she went to do the shopping she made careful enquiries at the post office, assuming correctly that they would have the information she was seeking, about the island's location and if any bus would take her anywhere near. She would have asked about the tides as well, just as a matter of interest, if this information had not been voluntarily given by the portly, bewhiskered postmaster who looked exactly like Mr Pickwick.

'You'll have to watch the tides, miss,' he told her solemnly. 'Can't cross at high tide and that's roughly twelve noon at this time of year. As far as I can recollect there's a notice by the causeway giving tidal information. And a warning.' He wagged a fat, pork-sausage-type finger at her. 'Oh, yes, not to be trifled with aren't high tides.'

Ashley already knew that to her cost and she thanked him.

Regarding transport he was much more jovial. 'There's a number 16 bus goes from right outside here. On the hour every even hour. Except Sundays and Bank Holidays. Goes right through to Thorpley village it does, but they'll put you off at the causeway if you ask them. Runs every hour, odd and even on Thursdays on account of that being Thorpley's market day.' He paused to draw breath and to vigorously stamp the pension book of an elderly customer. 'I'm just thinking, lass, that there's better places to go viewing than Troon Island. Even if the tide's in your favour, there'd be nowt for you to look at. And you wouldn't be welcome. Fine, upstanding young fellow is young Bradley Thornton but somewhat averse to visitors. But then that's his business, I always say. Now if you fancy a trip off ...' Having dispensed with his latest customer the postmaster was ready to act as tourist information officer for Ashley's benefit and she listened politely, but her mind was quite made up.

When she could finally get away she wondered if all Storrs' inhabitants were as talkative as the postmaster and little Milly France.

On Tuesday Andrea was much better

and made things easy for Ashley by telling her she had a long-standing engagement to give a talk and demonstration on cake-icing at the village WI that afternoon.

'Of course you're quite welcome to come along,' she said with a smile.

'No thank you,' Ashley told her, 'I'd love to see your demonstration, you really do amaze me, Andrea, but I rather thought I'd do a bit of exploring seeing as the weather's fairly good. Who knows, I might be a shopkeeper before long and won't get many opportunities to wander off. Could I make a packed lunch to take with me, do you think?'

'Of course. Help yourself.' Andrea left the kitchen to go and, as she put it, try to sort out the jumble sale on Peter's desk.

So, Ashley thought, she could take her time: catch the ten o'clock bus, Mr Pickwick said it was only about ten minutes' journey, and be at the causeway long before any high tide.

Of course, she added, as she got out the

breadknife, she wouldn't go across!

But she did.

When she stepped off the bus she found herself standing on the top of the cliffs with nothing in either direction but fields and the narrow, winding road with here and there a lone house, and in the distance, a church spire which could be Thorpley village. In front of her was the sea, which today was calm and sparkling in the pleasant though cold sunshine; and Troon Island, a fair distance out and not really an island at the moment because the cobbled causeway led safely and invitingly across. It was difficult at this distance to gauge the exact size of the island and it had a thick fringe of trees, which, even at this time of the year hid what might have been a good view of the Manor House. Close to the shore, however, Ashley could see the doll's house of a cottage. The present home of 'young Bradley Thornton', if she could believe what she had been told, and

109

there was no reason she shouldn't.

She could not see his boat so that was probably a good sign that he wasn't at home. Why should he be, on such a pleasant morning? Out with a fishing party more than likely.

There were rough-hewn steps set into the cliff face that led down on to the mainly pebbly beach. It was so quiet and peaceful. Ashley could hear only her own scrambling footsteps and the occasional scratch and scutter of a disturbed small rock or pebble as she made her descent of the steps.

She had the beach all to herself. The clear air was like wine and she flung out her arms and twirled around for the sheer joy of it. She felt good. A few short weeks ago she would never have believed she could be content living in a place like Storrs. At the very least she would have imagined having to do some serious re-adjustment after twenty-three years of city life, but there had been none of that.

She liked the silence of country fife. She liked the sea and the tang of it. At night she slept dreamlessly, and she was already developing a huge appetite.

She had her work in Milly's shop to look forward to and things could not have been better. Of course, she still missed her father sometimes, that was only natural, but both she and Andrea had known his release from pain and suffering had been a blessing. She did not miss Karl at all. And all this after just a few days! Who said village and country life was boring?

The causeway stretched ahead of her. The sea was far, far out. Miles out it seemed to her; she glanced at her watch. Still only 10.20. Plenty of time for her to go across there and back in safety. She only wanted to have a look—a quick exploration whilst the coast was clear. She laughed to herself at this idea. The coastline could not have been clearer. Not a boat or a sail on the horizon. Only a few sea birds borne along gracefully on air currents shared the peaceful morning with her.

The cobbled causeway was wide enough to take a motor vehicle, provided at some point you could get one down on to the beach in the first place. As she neared Troon Island—and it did not seem as far as she had imagined once she had set off—Ashley saw the cottage quite clearly and was alarmed to see smoke curling lazily up from the chimney. She hesitated. Smoke meant a fire and a fire meant habitation. Should she go on? She looked back the way she had come. If she turned back now she might never get another opportunity. Already her heart was beginning to thump, as though she had a reason to feel guilty, which was ridiculous; she was doing nothing wrong, but perhaps given time to reflect she might change her mind about visiting Troon Island again.

She continued on her journey across the causeway. If Brad Thornton was spying at her through his curtains then so be it, but nobody appeared at the cottage door and the cottage certainly looked empty. It was only when she was nearly there that she saw the car, the same one that Brad had driven her back to the vicarage in. Now she knew that there was a way down on to the beach for vehicles. The car was half-screened behind some bushes, but there was no mistaking it. So he was here. Somewhere. This knowledge made Ashley step out with an even firmer tread. If she was being watched she wasn't going to look guilty.

She stepped off the last of the cobbles on to firm ground. She glanced at her watch. 10.30. It had taken her about ten minutes. Whatever else she did, she must not forget the time.

There was a neat little cottage garden surrounded by a wooden fence. It had no air of dereliction about it. Paintwork was fresh. Curtains hung neatly at the small-paned windows. A path led directly past the cottage into a sort of copse of trees. Ashley took the path and soon found herself at the end of a long, smooth driveway. A pair of tall iron gates stood open. One was broken. The grass on either side of the drive was wild and full of weeds, but dry and dead-looking now because of the long, hot summer. Now the Manor was clearly visible. It was huge, built of grey stone, twin gables faced outwards on either side of tall stone chimneys. Even at a distance it was easy to see that the house was empty, un-lived in. Un-loved. Or was this purely Ashley's imagination because of the story Milly had told her? She started to walk nearer to the house, trying to imagine what it would have looked like in years gone by when the Thorntons lived here, generations of Thorntons bringing up their children, the house being handed down the family line till it reached Brad Thornton's father.

Because of him the house had fallen into disrepair. Because of him the most recent Thornton had been driven away and when he returned on his father's death, it was merely to occupy the small cottage, not the main house. For some reason known only to himself, he had not wanted to live there or, judging by the look of things, to carry out any repairs or maintenance. The gardens were jungles. A few windows were boarded up, the rest were sightless, soulless eyes staring at nothing, seeing nothing. Ashley had never seen anything sadder in her life.

She stood looking up at this huge, beautiful, dreadfully neglected house, thinking what a waste it was. She was lost in her own world of imagination; a dream-world of parties and bright lights; of laughter and voices; of warmth and friendliness. So lost that she did not hear the footsteps approaching nor see the way Brad Thornton, coming round from the back of the house, dropped the handles of a wheelbarrow as though they were red hot. She only came back to the present when he spoke to her.

'What the hell do you think you're doing here?'

Ashley almost jumped out of her skin. She swung round to face him. He was wearing an old brown sweater, corduroy trousers and wellington boots. Now that he wasn't wearing his silly peaked cap Ashley could see he had unruly hair that had a natural curl to it. He had dirty smudges on his forehead as though he had wiped it with a grimy hand. Once again his expression was hostile. He was also very angry.

As on their previous encounter, Ashley was immediately on the defensive.

'I'm just looking. No harm in that, is there?'

'Yes, there is. This is private property.'

'I didn't see any notice to that effect.'

'I don't need a notice. Everyone knows Troon Island is private.'

Ashley smiled tightly. 'I'm a newcomer. I'm not yet conversant with your quaint little ways.'

He moved a threatening step nearer.

Ashley in her turn backed away. Why was her heart beating so fast? Why had her mouth gone so dry? Surely she wasn't scared of this man. Of course she wasn't, but suddenly she was very much aware that there were just the two of them in the middle of nowhere.

'How did you get here?' he barked.

'I walked. From the bus-stop, anyway.'

Brad Thornton gave one of his unpleasant smiles. 'And why did you come? How did you even know this place existed if you're a "newcomer"?' Before Ashley could speak he rushed on sarcastically, 'Oh, of course, you're the vicar's sister-in-law, aren't you? I was forgetting. Going about "doing good" I suppose. Visiting the needy on the Reverend's behalf. Well you're not welcome here and neither is your bloody parson.'

It was now clear to Ashley that 'young Bradley Thornton' had a big chip on his shoulder about clergymen and anyone connected with them. Why? Was it something to do with his past, his departure from Storrs, his hermit-like existence here on Troon Island? As if she cared!

But even as she was prepared to toss her head and walk away from him, she realized that she did care, because suddenly in those deep, dark eyes she had caught a glimpse of something other than bitterness and sarcasm. It was gone as quickly as it came, but she had not mistaken the hurt that momentarily flashed there.

She decided once again to offer him an olive branch. Whether he took it or not was entirely up to him.

'As a matter of fact, I came to see you on my own behalf,' she began. 'It doesn't really matter how I knew you lived here, but I'd been down to the harbour a couple of times and your boat wasn't there. I wanted to try to thank you properly for saving my life. I realized I must have seemed less than grateful and I'm very sorry. I'm not usually rude and ill-mannered, but I was in shock, I suppose, scared too. Now I've had time to go over it all in my mind and ... well ... quite simply ... thank you!'

For a long moment there was silence. Only the noise of the seagulls and the gentle rustling of windblown leaves broke the silence. Brad pushed his hand through his hair and took another step towards her. This time Ashley did not back away. He came very close, his expression now was non-committal. If her heart beat any louder he must surely hear it, she thought.

It was going to be all right. He had accepted her peace offering. Any minute now he would smile, extend his hand perhaps. They could start again. They might even be friends.

Swiftly, before she had time to catch her breath, he had pulled her into his arms and was kissing her long and hard on the mouth. His hands gripped her shoulders tightly, hurting her, but she welcomed the pain as her mouth moved greedily beneath his own. When he finally released her she was speechless, still feeling the imprint of his hot, demanding lips, the pressure of his fingers. Why had he done that? And why wasn't she furious with him for daring to do it?

When she saw the beginnings of yet another slow, sarcastic smile Ashley realized she had entirely misinterpreted the kiss.

'Well now,' he drawled, 'you've thanked me properly, haven't you? So now we're equal, I think, and I suggest you begin your trip back across the causeway before I'm forced to rescue you yet again!'

Seven

Ashley said nothing about the incident to her sister. No one should ever know how humiliated she had felt; how awful it had been to go back across the causeway, feeling his eyes on her back, though that was probably her imagination. As far as she was aware, Brad Thornton had not followed her back through the copse. Only once she had gained the mainland did she turn to look back at Troon Island, viewing it through a haze of tears. It would probably be her last sight of the place. No way would she ever come this way again. She went to wait for the bus which seemed ages in arriving, but as she had never thought to ask about return bus times she had no option but to stand at the side of the road and wait. To make matters worse the bright, fresh morning was turning grey and cold. Ashley hoped the threatening rain would hold off, but was not really surprised when it didn't. She stood getting wetter and colder and feeling more miserable.

If only she could feel seething anger against that man, but she couldn't, and this was the worst thing of all, because she had enjoyed the kiss so much and would quite happily have stood there in his arms being kissed till the cows came home!

He had made it very plain to her why he had kissed her. She had even heard him laughing as she turned her back on him and walked away. It made no difference. Oh, she was a fine one! All those lofty ideas about never needing another man. Karl Whittaker had made her cry more than once and after their break-up Ashley had vowed no other man would ever make her cry again. Look at her now! Less than a week in Storrs and she was at it again.

The bus arrived at last and Ashley went

to sit by herself on the back seat, as far away from the few other passengers as she could get. The rain was dripping from her hair, trickling down her neck and she knew she looked a mess. She was sure, too, that everyone would be able to tell that not all the wetness on her face was from the rain. She got out her hankie and tried to wipe some of the wet away. When she opened her shoulder-bag to take out her pocket mirror she saw the packet of sandwiches she had prepared. She couldn't possibly have a picnic lunch now. She would have to go straight to the vicarage. At least the rain had given her an excuse to go back earlier than she had intended.

When she finally arrived and had begun to dry out, sitting near the Aga with a cup of hot, home-made soup, Andrea said delightedly, 'Now you'll be able to come to the WI with me, won't you?'

Ashley looked up vaguely. 'The WI?' she repeated, her mind still on Brad Thornton.

'The Women's Institute. The cake-icing demonstration.'

'Oh, yes.' She knew her voice lacked enthusiasm.

'Of course, you don't have to come,' Andrea said, 'if you think you might be bored.'

'Oh, Andrea, of course I won't be bored. Don't be silly. I'd love to come. Though perhaps I'd be better going to a cake-making demonstration seeing I can't bake to save my life!'

Andrea smiled. 'Sorry! The cake's already baked.'

When she was alone, feeling warmth returning to her hands and feet, Ashley told herself she must pull herself together. She had absolutely no reason to feel down in the dumps. No *valid* reason. Andrea was no fool, quite the reverse, and if she should suspect that Ashley was unhappy she would naturally want to know why. A person couldn't leave the house full of smiles and return a couple of hours later looking and feeling so terrible. Unless, of course, the person happened to have had an encounter with the most horrible, cruel, sarcastic, unfeeling monster who ever drew breath!

Ashley groaned aloud. Who was she trying to kid? Brad Thornton was all those things, and more; but knowing his faults, knowing she meant less than nothing to him, did not alter how she felt.

'It isn't possible!' she spoke aloud. 'It doesn't happen in real life.'

Andrea came back into the kitchen.

'Talking to yourself?' she said in a teasing voice.

Ashley gave a little laugh. 'The first sign of madness, don't they say?'

She got up and put her empty mug on the sink. 'I think I'll get changed. What time do we have to go?'

'Oh, not till about two and we've only to go as far as the village hall. The meeting starts at half-past but I want to set up shop first.'

Ashley went slowly upstairs. The first sign of madness, and goodness knew she *was* mad. She must be to have fallen in love with Bradley Thornton! When she first met Karl she had thought he was handsome and charming and he had done his utmost to flirt with her, but her feelings for him had come gradually over many weeks, if not months. In the beginning, Karl had looked at no one but her and when Ashley did first realize she cared for him, their relationship for a short while had been idyllic. She had told herself it was true love. Perhaps it had been, but time had soured her love and she and Karl, for various reasons, had grown apart. But even on that last, bitter evening when she had watched him walk away from the flat, away from her, the hurt had been deep and real, the desolate ache for love lost, for an unfulfilled vision of what might have been, tangible enough to wound her.

In less than a week in this small and quaint Yorkshire village, Karl was but a hazy memory. As Ashley got out fresh, dry jeans she tried to imagine Karl's face, how his kisses, his lovemaking had made her feel. But she couldn't. Oh, she could remember the pain, that was easy, but not the love. There was no room in her heart now for Karl. Brad Thornton had taken complete possession of it.

She pulled off her creased, cotton trousers and flung them in exasperation against the wardrobe door. It wasn't fair. She had been so happy. She could cheerfully have spent the next twenty or thirty years moseying along, running Milly's shop, getting to know people, helping to bring up Andrea's baby. She would have made a lovely spinster aunt! She probably still would, she realized wryly, as Bradley Thornton was not going to change her situation!

Whatever she might feel for him he had nothing but contempt and loathing for her. Why couldn't her own feelings, so healthily begun, have developed further along those lines? Why did the contempt have to change to caring and the loathing to longing?

She completed her change of clothing and dragged a comb through her short, brown hair. Her hair was one of her less favourite attributes. Unlike Andrea's which grew soft and curly and very feminine, Ashley's had to be kept really short, otherwise nature would run rampant and her hair would spring out thickly all around her face. Sometimes she longed for long, silky tresses; only once had she given in to this longing. The results were so disastrous, long before she had achieved her goal of shoulder-length hair, that she had never attempted it again. Karl, amongst others, had told her her hair suited her short and she would have been displaying false modesty to think she wasn't attractive, but still she got those envious twinges, especially now when she was feeling sorry for herself in the first place. Then, as she looked at herself in the dressing-table mirror, she could not help comparing her own hair with Brad Thornton's. The same colour, the same texture. His did run rampant and could not have argued against the idea of a thorough brushing.

Brad. Again, after a too-brief respite, he was at the forefront of her thoughts. He had kissed her once in a way that promised no affection. Could one kiss do all this to her? Create the ache, the longing, the ... hurt? Of course it couldn't and she would not fool herself any longer. The kiss had only been a culmination of her aroused feelings. From the first moment she had laid eyes on Brad Thornton she had been deeply attracted to him; sensually aware of him. That was why she had had to keep telling herself that no man had a chance of entering her life again. At least not for a very long time.

"Methinks the lady doth protest too much", she thought. At all costs, neither Andrea nor Peter must be aware of how she felt. She did not think for one minute that her sister was a gossip, but Ashley was taking no chances. Storrs was a small place, and Ashley was sure Milly France was not the only person living there who knew everyone and everything. Ashley dare not think how terrible it would be if word somehow got back to Brad Thornton that she liked him.

Andrea called out from the bottom of the stairs and quickly Ashley moved away from the dressing-table, ready to face the good ladies of the Storrs branch of the WI.

Within three weeks Ashley was installed in Milly's shop. The weather had turned bitterly cold as November came, with frequent sea frets that kept boats, including Brad Thornton's, safely moored in the harbour. The season, of course, was now well and truly over and business in the shop was far from brisk. After, that is, the first few days, when all and sundry found their way inside the little building, sometimes to browse, sometimes to buy, but Ashley knew, mainly to view her. And, she was sure, to make her feel welcome. The lack of buying customers did not bother her. Milly had warned her to expect nothing else until much nearer Christmas when seasonal trade would pick up until perhaps the middle of January. Ashley, eager to start off on the right foot, welcomed all Milly's advice and help. She opened the shop Mondays, Wednesdays and Fridays from 10.00 am to 4.00 pm and Saturday mornings from 9.00 am to noon. In the spring and summer she would be prepared to open for much longer hours as and when custom demanded that she did so.

Having few customers did not mean that she was bored or had time on her hands. She spent a great deal of time checking and sorting out all the many and varied stock items, frequently coming across items of particular interest, a magazine or a book, even old-fashioned items like wooden jigsaws and bags of glass marbles that must have been there for ever and a day. She re-arranged stock, she dusted and washed wooden shelves and the glass cabinet that stood on the wide wooden counter housing most of the jewellery; beads, bracelets, brooches—nothing of great value but some really pretty pieces—and, of course, the unusual silver rings. It was an Aladdin's cave which Ashley was certain she would never tire of exploring.

At the end of the day she would lock up and walk back to the vicarage, feeling proud of herself, especially if she had sold quite a few things. When she passed people on the street they would smile and greet her. Some stopped to pass the time of day or to remark on the weather. It was a good life. Most evenings were spent in the warmth of the vicarage, reading or playing Scrabble with Andrea and Peter, when he had an evening off, that is. It was amazing how busy his small country parish kept him. They had a TV, but did not watch it much. Ashley preferred to help Andrea with her baking, determined to learn how to turn out a batch of fluffy scones or an egg custard where the pastry did not rise to the top. She was also learning how to knit. How her childhood had been neglected, she thought, and remembered guiltily how she had never had the time or patience with knitting or sewing needles, whilst Andrea, from a very early age, had been skilled with both.

With the approach of winter various evening activities were starting up in Storrs: a Gardening Club—neither Ashley nor Andrea's cup of tea!; a Drama Group which Ashley was undecided about joining. She could not act to save her life but she would not mind working behind the scenes. There were groups, too, specifically affiliated to St Mark's church. The Women's Society for one, who met every second Tuesday night for social get-togethers, guest speakers on many different topics and what was amusingly called a 'Knit and Natter Evening' when coloured squares were turned out by the dozen, afterwards to be sewn together to make blankets for the Third World countries. Ashley was no use at all on the practical side of his venture, but she did volunteer to make the tea and coffee for the other industrious workers!

Keeping busy, tiring herself out so that she slept well at nights was, she knew, the best thing for her. To try to keep thoughts of Brad Thornton at bay was her main objective. It wasn't easy. His boat in the harbour alone was a constant reminder. Of course she did not have to look at it; she did not have to gaze along the quayside every time she came down to the shop, to see if she could catch a glimpse of Brad. She did not have to look up with her heart in her mouth every time anybody came into the shop. As if he would come in. Why on earth should he? What use would a man like Bradley Thornton have for the trinkets and gee-gaws she sold?

Because she had 'pooh-poohed' this preposterous idea so many times, the sight of him that cold, foggy Wednesday morning was all the more shocking. It did not help to still her terrified heartbeats that Brad was already in the shop when she arrived. The door ajar was the first sign that something was amiss and with the word 'Burglary' in her head, Ashley pushed the door fully open and there he was, standing at the back of the counter with her newly replenished First Aid box in his hand—Milly had merely had half a packet of out-dated headache tablets and a couple of strips of plaster. He was holding up his left hand, from which blood was dripping on to the counter.

The expression on his face suggested he was just as shocked to see her as she was to see him. Tossing aside the thought that Brad had more than likely cut his hand breaking into the shop, Ashley rushed over to the counter.

'Your hand!' she cried. 'You're bleeding.'

'How observant of you!' Brad said sardonically. Even now with his life's blood ebbing away he could not be pleasant. 'Do you happen to know where Milly is?' As he spoke he was one-handedly removing a wad of cotton wool from the box and pressing it to the wound on his thumb.

'I've no idea,' Ashley said. 'How did you get in here? Customers usually stay this side of the counter.'

She pushed up the counter's flap and joined him on the other side.

'I'm not a customer. I've come to get a bloody plaster. I've cut my wretched thumb.'

'No! I wouldn't have noticed.' Ashley could be as sarcastic as he was. 'Here, let me do that.' She took the cotton wool from him. 'You'd better go into the kitchen. You're making a mess in here.'

To her surprise he allowed himself to be led into the tiny washroom-cum-kitchenette and for a few moments whilst

Ashley tended to his cut thumb—purely superficial—neither of them spoke. Then, of course, they both spoke together.

He said, 'You seem to know your way about.'

And she said, 'May I ask how you got in here?'

Then they both stared at one another and Brad said, 'I came through the door. I have a key. A key that Milly gave me. I know it might sound stupid but I couldn't find a piece of sticking-plaster to bless myself with on board my boat. So I came around here.' He paused, leaving the confinement of the kitchen for the only slightly less confining area behind the counter. Ashley looked at the blood and went back to get a cloth.

'And now it's your turn,' Brad continued, leaning casually against the counter.

'My turn?' she repeated.

'To explain yourself.'

'This is my shop.' Ashley enjoyed seeing the surprise on his face.

'Since when?' he asked.

'Since just over a week ago. I bought it from Milly. The stock, that is, I'm only leasing the shop.'

'She didn't tell me.'

'Any reason why she should?'

'None. Except she's my godmother and I visit her regularly. I knew she'd been trying to sell the shop, but nothing about you.'

He emphasized the last word as though he found the idea of her owning Milly's shop distasteful. If Ashley had nursed any thoughts of Brad Thornton turning out to be half-way human she was in for a disappointment. He wasn't even going to thank her for the plaster. She wondered why Milly had not mentioned being Brad's godmother. She had made out she knew little or nothing about what he was doing since he came back to Storrs. Why would she want to do that? It didn't make sense.

'Perhaps I could have your key.' Ashley held out her hand. She was feeling extremely uncomfortable standing so close to him.

His face set grimly as he dug into his trouser pocket and produced a key, almost flinging it at her.

'With pleasure!' He moved past her, their bodies touching as Brad made his way from behind the counter and across to the door. Ashley almost called out, 'Brad, don't go. I'm sorry,' but held back the words. She was sure any entreaty she made would only bring forth another sarcastic remark, another sardonic look.

Then he was gone, banging the door behind him. Ashley watched him stride off through the mist towards the harbour.

Oh, how stupid, there were tears in her eyes. She cleared up the rest of the mess and put on the kettle to make some tea. She was shaking. What was the matter with her? And why had she continually to keep bumping into that man? It seemed as though their paths were fated to cross. And whenever they did, they inevitably crossed swords. They had declared war on one another on that first encounter. Ashley could not honestly envisage their ever being able to be friends, let alone anything more.

And because she knew that at each subsequent meeting she stupidly and irrationally lost a little bit more of her heart to Brad Thornton, Ashley could only feel very despondent about the future.

Eight

It was the third week in November when the winter gales for which Storrs was noted began in earnest. Sometimes the wind was so fierce only those who had to ventured out of doors. With the wind came icy, lashing rain and even flurries of snow or hailstones which stung the cheeks and took away the breath. Consequently Ashley was obliged to reduce the opening hours of her shop. There was no point in battling down to the harbour front when few, if any, customers would appear on her doorstep.

She had quite a decent view of the wild, surging, relentless sea from the upstairs windows at the vicarage, and sometimes she felt frightened; the sea seemed so rough and out of control and she could not help thinking about Troon Island and wondering if Brad was still living out there. If he wasn't, where did he stay in such atrocious weather? He couldn't, she was sure, use his boat to come and go in, and wouldn't the causeway be impassable, too risky even for a local, with such unpredictable tides?

Peter came and went much the same as usual. 'Doing the Lord's work' as he cheerfully put it. Swathed in scarf, woolly hat, gloves, waterproof jacket and boots, he left the vicarage most days whatever the weather, sometimes not returning till late evening, glowing with cold; Ashley could feel the chill of his breath, face and hands from the other side of the room. Andrea would rush to help him off with his outdoor clothes, fetch his slippers, bring him a hot drink. Ashley looked on in envy. When the weather was at its worst and Peter had gone further afield, say to Scarborough or Whitby, both towns a fair distance from Storrs and having open, desolate moors to cross to get to

Whitby, Ashley sensed that her sister was very much on edge until Peter returned safely. Andrea never voiced her concern, but she would act out of character, restless and nervy, her needlework or sewing lying idle in her hands.

Confinement to the house left Ashley with too much time for thoughts. It didn't help that Milly was away for a few days visiting a relative in York. Ashley longed to be able to talk to her about Brad. Well, at least to try to find out why Milly had not mentioned their relationship. If Brad was her godson and in his own words 'visited. her frequently' surely it would have been the most natural thing in the world to tell him about the change of ownership of the shop. Yet she had said nothing, neither to Brad nor to Ashley. And Ashley realized now that Milly had been very vague and generalizing when she talked about Brad and his father. There had been no hint whatsoever that she knew the Thornton family on any more intimate terms than the rest of Storrs. But she must have done.

Ashley was intrigued to say the least and knew as soon as Milly came home she would have to talk to her. She realized that by doing so she would leave herself wide open for speculation and gossip about her feelings for Brad. She was beyond caring. Let Milly—let any of them—read into it what they would. She did love Bradley Thornton anyway, so let them bandy that idea around as much as they wanted.

But then she thought—what if the story reached Brad's ears as it must surely do sooner or later? Oh, it was all so confusing. Sometimes Ashley paced up and down her bedroom like a caged lion. The weather was beginning to get on her nerves. She longed to be out and about. Oh, for some cold, crisp days so that she could go for a walk, breathe in the sea air, clear her head. But the high winds and the gales continued with no sign of a let up and December nearly upon them. Then it would be Christmas before they knew where they were. It was too much to hope for snow 'deep and crisp and even' but couldn't there be just a tiny indication that the weather would be more seasonal!

'Are you coming to the Women's Society meeting this afternoon?' Andrea asked on the following Tuesday morning.

Ashley looked up from where she was tackling the breakfast washing up.

'Is it still going ahead? Do you think anyone will bother to turn up? I mean, look at it!' She nodded towards the window where the windblown rain was lashing, making it almost impossible to see out of it.

'Oh, they'll turn up all right,' Andrea declared with a slow, mysterious sort of smile. 'We're having a special guest speaker. The one we booked can't make it. 'Flu or something, but a replacement's been found. He's giving a talk on Italy with coloured slides.'

It sounded boring and Ashley was in no

mood to be bored. She could feel that way by herself, thank you; she did not need any assistance.

'What's so special about this man?' she asked, pulling out the plug, watching the soap suds gurgle down the plughole.

'He lived in Italy for a number of years and by all accounts he's very interesting.'

Really, Ashley thought listlessly, wondering when the rain was going to stop. Oh, well, she may as well go with Andrea. She had a soft spot for Italy, having spent holidays in both Tuscany and Sorrento. The latter with Karl. Perhaps that was a reason for not going. Wouldn't hurtful memories be stirred up? Wasn't she feeling low enough?

She made a determined effort to be cheerful. Andrea seemed full of high spirits, singing as she did her housework. She had got over her queasy stomach and was blooming with good health and did not seem to be too concerned about the weather.

As they reached the parish hall adjoining the church where the Women's Society had their meetings, Ashley could immediately tell that very few of the women were put out by the wind and the rain, laughing and talking as they shook out their umbrellas and hung up their raincoats. The hall was warm; Peter had made sure the heating was switched on first thing that morning.

Andrea and Ashley were greeted by everyone, and Ashley knew suddenly that *her* low spirits were nothing whatsoever to do with the weather. It could have been brilliant sunshine outside and she would still have felt miserable; but she did try, and pushed all thoughts of Brad Thornton out of her mind. At least until, as she went with Andrea into the kitchen to start setting out the cups and saucers, she heard one of the women say to her friend, 'Oh, yes, you could have knocked me down with a feather. Well, we were all surprised, weren't we? Somebody must have some influence that's all I can say to get young Bradley Thornton here today.'

Ashley froze and she almost dropped the pile of saucers she was holding.

'Bradley Thornton?' She swung round but the two women were already leaving the kitchen and did not hear her. Andrea did and when she gave Ashley a wide, innocent smile Ashley cried out, 'You knew as well, didn't you? That's why you wanted me to come here. Was it you who asked him?'

'No, no, it was Milly France,' Andrea said.

'She's in York.'

'I know, but I phoned her. Oh, it's a long story.'

Ashley crashed the saucer on to the table. 'I'm listening,' she said stoutly.

Andrea admitted to having met Milly a couple of weeks ago and having a cup of tea with her. Brad's name came up in conversation, Milly telling Andrea about her relationship with Brad. She also told her he had a wonderful collection of slides on Italy which might be a good idea to keep in mind.

'So naturally,' Andrea concluded, 'when Mr Potter gave backword at the last minute, I thought of Brad and got in touch with Milly and she did the rest.'

Ashley felt highly suspicious. Should she admit to her sister that she knew Milly France was Brad's godmother or should she give the impression she was hearing the information for the first time? Why hadn't Andrea told her she and Milly had met? And why had Milly been so forthcoming with Andrea but not with herself?

Andrea was behaving too, too innocently but Ashley was not convinced. There was some sort of conspiracy in force. Milly France and Andrea were in on it and who else, for goodness' sake? Surely Brad himself did not, could not, realize he was being manipulated. If he did, wouldn't he have run a mile rather than come here today? Why would he come at all? He had little or no time for the Church. He was a loner. Soon she and Brad would come face to face and what good would it do either of them?

There was an air of buzzing excitement in the hall as the assembled women took their seats. From choice Ashley would have sat at the very back but Andrea got hold of her arm and manoeuvred her to the front.

'I've got to welcome Mr Thornton,' she said in mitigation. He had his back to them setting up his screen and slide-projector. He was wearing a suit and when he turned Ashley's legs turned to jelly at the sight of him. His shirt was crisp and white, his tie a deep dark red. He had had his hair cut and looked nothing like the sea-farer she had first met or the windblown man with the wheelbarrow on Troon Island. He was smiling, too. First at Andrea then at her. Either he was a very good actor or he really was pleased to see them.

'Good afternoon, Mrs Winford. Miss Elliott,' he said. Then to the assembled company, 'Good afternoon ladies.'

They simpered and they giggled like schoolgirls. They lapped up his every word and gesture whilst Ashley sat willing her thumping heart to slow down.

It was an interesting afternoon, and Brad's accompanying talk was witty and informative. If Ashley did not know what he was really like, how he had sneered at Peter and the Church, she would have thought Bradley Thornton the most charming man she had ever met. Could Milly really have so much influence with him, persuading him to come here as a guest-speaker? The women loved him, even Andrea, and afterwards when a vote of thanks had been given and tea and biscuits were served, they swarmed around him, bombarding him with questions, all of which he answered politely and patiently. Ashley could not believe what she was seeing and hearing.

Then suddenly she caught his glance. She had retired to the back of the hall to drink her tea alone, there to watch and listen and feast her eyes on him, whilst she ached to be alone with him and have him smile at her as he was at all the others. When he looked directly at her, the warm smile wavered and Ashley realized it did not and had not ever, all the afternoon, reached his eyes. It *was* an act. The coldness, the bitterness was still there. Why? Was it just dislike of her? And why did he dislike her? Could he be the sort of man to bear a grudge for ever because she had been foolish enough to get trapped on the rocks?

She lifted her cup to her lips and all the time they watched one another. A large woman standing near him tugged possessively at his arm. She had a voice as large as her framework and it carried.

'Now, Mr Thornton, it's been a real pleasure getting to know you. Fancy you pretending to be a hermit, shutting yourself away. You won't do it again, will you? We shall expect to see a lot more of you. And there's another thing!' The large woman had moved even closer to him, still holding on to his arm, beaming at him in what she must surely believe was a motherly way. 'Isn't it high time you got yourself a wife and opened up that big house of yours again?'

There seemed to be a long, dreadful pause. The crowd of women were waiting for Brad to speak. Ashley, even from a distance, was probably the only one who saw the tension come to his face; who noted the paling of his cheeks. With a deliberate movement Brad removed the questioner's fingers from his arm in such a way that she gave a little gasp and took a step backwards. The light, bantering tone had completely gone from his voice as he said, 'I am willing, madam, to answer all your questions about Italy, my hobbies, my prowess as a photographer, my boat, even to tell you what I eat for breakfast; but my personal, private life is my own and I should like to keep it that way. Excuse me.' He turned from the throng who allowed him, some of them standing open-mouthed in amazement, to pass through them to where he had left all his equipment, which he gathered up and then made his way to the exit.

So, Ashley thought he had not been able to keep up his pleasantness. It had only been possible for a couple of hours at the most. Now the women were talking amongst themselves Ashley could hear their 'Well, I never', and their 'Who does he think he is, the young upstart?' When Andrea emerged from the kitchen, they swarmed around her voicing their complaints.

Ashley decided to go back to the vicarage alone, unable to bear hearing Brad pulled to pieces, thinking irreverently how quickly 'Hosanna!' could become 'Crucify'! As she emerged from the hall, not even telling Andrea she was going, she saw Brad swerving off through the pouring rain, driving like a madman. He saw her, looking straight at her. He did not, of course, acknowledge her.

Once again as on that day on the island, she was aware of the hurt, sad look in his eyes. She made up her mind, once and for all. When Milly got back she was going to find out just what exactly was eating Bradley Thornton.

In the first week of December, miraculously the bad weather eased off. No one knew at the time that this return to dry, cold weather was merely a lull, a seasonal interlude, a calm before the storm. Everyone welcomed the change. The sky was a pale winter-blue and most days the sun shone. It was very cold, but a healthy, bracing cold. There were morning frosts, breath turned to steam at the first venture out of doors and extra woollens were dragged from cupboards and drawers.

Andrea was now nearly six months pregnant and beginning to show. Peter teased her, pretending to have difficulty passing her if they should meet in a doorway, telling Ashley how his wife was gradually easing him out of their bed. Andrea took it all in good part, promising Peter that he had not seen anything yet!

Ashley got her meeting with Milly as soon as she knew Milly was home. She arrived unannounced one evening, believing that taking Milly by surprise was better than allowing her to prepare herself for the visit. Milly opened the door to her, ushering her inside, beaming with pleasure, but Ashley with the questions she wanted to ask rising up inside her, did not let Milly have chance to do more than put on the kettle before she said, 'Why didn't you tell me you were Brad Thornton's godmother?'

Milly continued to busy herself, setting out teacups and saucers, getting the milk out of the fridge. Ashley stood in the kitchen doorway watching her.

'Did your sister tell you that?' Milly asked.

'No. Brad did.'

Milly turned to look at her. She seemed surprised. 'You've seen Brad? Spoken to him? Recently, I mean?'

'Once or twice,' Ashley admitted. 'He came into the shop, seeking first aid. He was very surprised to see me there.'

Milly laughed, not in the least put out because Ashley had challenged her. The kettle came to the boil and Milly poured the water into the teapot.

'He would be! Come on, let's go sit down. I'm just ready for a cuppa.'

She gathered the items on to a wooden tray and preceded Ashley into the sitting-room.

'Are you going to answer my question?' Ashley persisted, determined not to be put off.

'Of course,' Milly said. 'If you remember when you first came here you asked me about Brad. Whether I knew him.'

'Yes, I did,' Ashley agreed, accepting a cup of tea, 'and you said you knew him *and* his family and you proceeded to tell me all about their history on Troon Island, but you didn't say you knew the Thorntons well enough to be Bradley Junior's godmother.'

'No, I didn't. And I had my reasons then.' Milly's face was the most serious Ashley had ever seen it. For once she seemed at a loss for words. That did not matter to Ashley. She had to have an answer.

'What reasons?' she said. Her tea was untouched.

Milly sipped her own tea slowly in a way that seemed to irritate Ashley.

'Looking back, I suppose it was silly of me, but I thought I was doing the right thing. Both for you. And Bradley.'

Ashley's puzzlement grew. Also her impatience. Milly was spinning out her answer. It was plain she did not want to give a direct answer at all.

'Please, Milly,' she begged, 'don't play cat and mouse with me.'

A sudden smile lit up Milly's kind face.

She was the old Milly again. 'I can see it's important to you, Ashley love. I can see Brad's important to you too.'

Ashley reddened and she looked away. 'What do you mean?' she faltered.

'Oh, love, it was plain as the nose on your face from the very first time you mentioned his name so casually. And you see, I knew it was important to Brad, too. I knew about you from him on that same day he rescued you from the rocks. Oh, he might have been able to fool other people by the disparaging, off-hand way he talked about you, but not me. Not Milly France.'

If her heart beat any faster, Ashley was sure it would burst right out of her body and fly away from her like a frightened bird.

Milly went on, 'I'd already met you in my shop, of course, but when I met you again and asked you to have tea with me, I could see why Brad should have fallen in love with you.'

Ashley gasped. 'Oh, he can't have,' she stammered, hoping, hoping so desperately that he had.

'I know what I'm talking about.' Milly spoke quietly. 'But I pretended to you that Bradley was no closer to me than to anybody else. I didn't want to do or say anything that would influence you one way or the other. I preferred to let nature take its course, but it seems to me now that doing that's going to take till doomsday.'

Still Ashley did not speak, for the simple reason that she could not think of anything to say. Milly leaned towards her and patted her hand gently.

'I persuaded Brad to come to your Women's Society but he told me he left on a sour note. He also told me he saw you on Troon Island and he was rude to you.'

It was on the tip of Ashley's tongue to say, 'Did he tell you he kissed me?' but she didn't. Surely Brad could not have mentioned that. Instead she whispered,

'Does Brad tell you everything?'

'No, not everything. Some things I have to find out for myself. Sometimes I have to use my intuition. Some things I guess at. Pure guesswork.'

'For instance?' Ashley was finding her voice at last. Here they were, discussing Brad Thornton, the man she loved. Was it possible, could it be possible that Milly was right about him? That he loved her too? He had done nothing, said nothing that in the slightest way indicated that he did. But then, had she? They were at each other's throats as soon as they met.

'I don't know why he shuts himself away like he does. I don't know why he has such black, despairing moods. I don't know for the life of me why he can't come straight out and "court" you as any normal, red-blooded man would do. I know he wants to. I can only guess at the reasons why he doesn't and looking at your face right now, Ashley, my dear, I am really sorry I haven't told you all this sooner, instead of being such a fool as to pretend half I knew about Bradley Thornton was from hearsay and gossip. What was I thinking of? Partly, as I said earlier it was because I didn't want to seem pushy. I didn't want to put words into Brad's mouth as it were, so I pretended ignorance about him and how he felt. But I'll tell you this now, I think he may have been married and had a child.'

A little feeling of fear came over Ashley. Married? Brad married?

'What makes you think that?' Her voice was no more than a squeak.

'I found a photograph. It fell out of his pocket. Soon after he came back from Italy. The photo was of a young woman holding a child of about eight or nine months. The woman looked Italian. I didn't mention it to Brad. Even as far back as five years ago when he came back to Storrs he was strange, distant.'

'Do you think he may have been married and divorced?'

Milly looked at her for a long, quiet minute. 'Or widowed.'

Suddenly Ashley knew it was true. Hadn't the hurt and pain rushed to Brad's eyes when the woman at the church-hall asked why he didn't get married? And if he had lost his wife, where was the child, who by now would be at least five years of age?

'I couldn't ask him,' Milly was saying, 'he comes and he goes here. Sometimes he's here every day. Sometimes I don't see him for weeks. I know what I can ask him and what I can't. I know it's been five years, but I can't rush him. And that's why, when he talked about you, Ashley, it gladdened me because he needs someone and you're so right for him.'

For a moment Ashley too felt gladdened. 'Am I?'

'Do you think you can handle him? It won't be easy. You've already learned how unapproachable he is and I'm proving to be a very poor match-maker.' Milly paused, then said in an odd sort of voice, 'Not like that other time. I was a great success then. Oh, a great success!'

Ashley had never heard bitterness in Milly's voice before, but it was there now.

What else did Milly still have to tell her? This was turning into a surprising evening.

Nine

In bed that night Ashley went over in her mind what Milly had told her. Picturing her at eighteen years old, fresh home from the ladies' secretarial college to where she had won a scholarship. A bright, intelligent girl of good, working-class stock who in the years before World War Two had been intent on becoming a secretary and had worked hard to get the coveted scholarship. At that time Milly's parents had owned the little shop, which in those days had been a general hardware store. Then came that fateful summer when young Milly had brought a friend home for the holidays. A dear friend, they were inseparable, though Emily Granger came from a wealthy family who lived in the south of England. Emily had needed no scholarship to get her into the college. For her, money had been enough. No matter. She and Milly became as close as two sisters and Milly was always made welcome at the Grangers' Surrey home.

At that time the parents of Bradley Thornton Senior lived on Troon Island, as well known, as popular as later Bradley himself became. He was two years older than Milly and already she was a regular visitor to Troon Island in the holidays. She worshipped Bradley from afar, but to him she was just a friend, someone to rag and tease, someone to invite to parties, to converse with on a variety of topics. The Thorntons had no edge to them and before the War parties at the Manor House were regular, well-attended by both rich and working class. It must have been a lovely way to live, Ashley realized, in the days when usual class-consciousness was the norm.

In the course of time Milly introduced her friend Emily to Bradley Thornton. It was love at first sight. By the end of that summer Emily and Bradley had publicly declared their love, Emily's parents had visited Troon Island and the young couple were engaged. Poor Milly stayed quietly, heartbrokenly in the background, happy for her friends, devastated for herself. She had never hoped, of course, to win Bradley's love for herself, but to lose him so quickly to her best friend ...

As it happened, and as was common in those days, Emily and Bradley had a long engagement, marrying finally in 1942 when, of course, England was at war. The war changed most people's lives. Emily's husband served in the Army as an officer and they were parted for many months. Then they were childless for years till, to their great joy, Bradley Junior was born in late 1955, ten years after the war ended: a war that claimed the life of Milly's father and brought her back to Storrs from her well-paid job in Cheltenham, to help support her mother, who never really recovered from her husband's death, and to run the shop. So it was that Milly's career came to an abrupt end, but she assured Ashley that she had no regrets, no bitterness, because after Emily and Bradley had been introduced, ironically Milly never settled away from Storrs again and was finally glad of an excuse to come back.

Young Bradley was born and Milly was asked to be godmother, which she did proudly and willingly. She remained Emily and Bradley's friend and never let them know her true feelings. But she never ever met anyone else to whom she could give her love and Ashley thought this was very sad.

When little Bradley was seven, Emily died from some sudden and rare blood disorder. The rest of the story Ashley knew. Now, too, she knew that Bradley had been intent on returning to Troon Island after his father died. He had returned, but not, Ashley was sure in the way he had intended. She became more and more convinced that his wife had died, perhaps in an accident, perhaps as the result of some sudden illness, as his own mother had. And like his own father before him, his wife's death had affected him deeply. And what of the child? Had Bradley, again like his father, deserted his own child?

She felt she must find out but Milly had told her everything she knew, concluding her story by saying, 'I lost Bradley to my best friend. I never blamed either of them. How could I? Bradley never knew how I felt and Emily certainly didn't. But I don't want you to lose Bradley's son, Ashley. I wish I could wave a magic wand over the pair of you and make everything all right, but I can't. I can only pray. Anything more positive must come from you and Brad.'

At the time she had left Milly's cottage, Ashley had been full of confidence, those fine, inspiring word ringing in her ears. It had seemed so simple. All she had to do was to meet Brad, on some neutral ground, to have a chance to start again, to say, 'I love you' and, if Milly's intuition was right, to hear Bradley say in return, 'I love you too.'

But later, lying in her darkened bedroom in the middle of the night when it seemed the whole world slept except herself, things did not seem so cut and dried. In the first place, how did she make contact with Brad? He was never there! It was true that Milly herself seemed to have an uncanny way of not only being able to see him, to speak to him, but of getting him to do as she wanted. If only Milly did have that magic wand she had mentioned.

Ashley's mind went back to the day she had visited Troon Island. She remembered now that Brad had been pushing a wheelbarrow round the side of the house. A wheelbarrow laden, she now recalled, with rubble, stones, dirt, pieces of wood. He had obviously been working at something. The grounds perhaps? The Manor House itself? Was he, could he, be starting some sort of renovations, and if so, surely there must only be one reason? He must be intending to move back into the Manor House. It had been empty for at least five years and badly neglected prior to that when Bradley Senior lived there alone after the death of his wife. Brad had been back at Storrs for a long time, up till now apparently quite content to live on his boat or in the cottage. Ashley realized she may be way off the mark in her assumption that he was finally setting about undoing the harm that had been inflicted on that beautiful old house, but somehow she did not think so. So why, why was he doing it?

She must visit the island again. She must take a closer look at the house knowing what she now knew. Perhaps there were workmen there; there must be too much for Brad to tackle alone. It could not be anyone local. That sort of news would spread like wildfire, but if Brad had gone further afield ...

Ashley smiled to herself as at last she settled down to sleep. If she wasn't careful she would be endowing the house with a complete new interior, sparkling chandeliers, wide-sweeping staircases, rich carpets and curtains. She had to hold her imagination in check. Otherwise she would be envisaging far more: herself as Brad's wife and mistress of the Manor House.

The cold, clear weather continued, for the present. Once again Ashley took the ten o'clock bus out to the causeway, telling nobody where she was going. She crossed to Troon Island and did not know whether to be glad or sorry that no smoke was rising from the cottage's chimney, or that Brad's car was not parked outside. There was a sort of eerie silence, no wind stirred the trees, no seagulls swooped and screeched and Ashley was unnerved. She felt like what she was—a trespasser who had no right to be there. But she was determined that nothing should deter her and marched through the copse, the crisp, hard leaf-strewn ground crackling and rustling beneath her feet. The house loomed ahead of her. So forlorn. So deserted. This time, with any luck, she would be able to get nearer, take a much closer look around.

When she did, she almost wished she had not, because closer inspection revealed broken windows, peeling paintwork, heart-breaking neglect that would surely cost a great deal of money and time to put right. Outside the big double doors, steps ran down on to a gravel terrace. Weeds had found their way between cracks and crevices, the steps themselves were broken in places. The windows were thick with grime and dirt.

As she was now positive that she was the only person on Troon Island, Ashley walked along the terrace intending to explore round the back of the house. Here the conditions were even worse: a garden cluttered and choked by weeds and dead grass; young trees with bent, broken branches. There was a privet hedge, too, overgrown of course, effectively hiding what lay beyond it.

Before venturing further Ashley peered through one or two of the windows, rubbing away at the dirt in order to see through the glass. She was amazed to see that there was still furniture inside. She was looking into what could have been a breakfast-room. It contained a heavy, dark round table and chairs, a matching Welsh dresser, still holding dishes and pots, a carpet faded and dusty-looking which could have been a warm rust-red when clean.

The next window gave her a good view of the kitchen. The units were old-fashioned; some had doors half-opened and the sink under the window was badly stained. The tiled floor should have been black and white.

Idiotically, Ashley felt tears pricking her eyes, a feeling of depression coming over her at the sight of all that abandonment and neglect. She had no heart to see any more and quickly turned away from the house to pick her way through the overgrown kitchen garden towards the high privet hedge. She pushed open the wooden gate set in the hedge, which creaked and groaned on its precariously hanging hinges. Beyond the hedge was open land which should, if properly maintained, have been lovely, but which now only matched the rest of the house and gardens. Beyond the open land was the sea. The other side of Troon Island. A haven of peace, a precious gem set in a silver sea. How much happiness had this place known? How much love? How much laughter? And later, how much sadness, how many tears?

On the still, quiet air came the sound of a car's engine. Ashley turned back towards the gate. Brad must be arriving! Should she hide and hope she would have an opportunity to escape across the causeway? Or should she stay and face him? This was her chance, probably the last opportunity she would have to put Milly's theory to the test. Resolutely Ashley pushed open the gate and stepped through so she would be in full view of the house and anyone who approached it or went inside. She clearly heard the engine switching off, the opening and shutting of the door, Brad's footsteps as he approached the house. Then silence. She stood listening intently. Where had he gone? She was feeling jittery and when Brad suddenly loomed up at the kitchen window, Ashley let out a yelp of surprise, jumping violently. She did not miss the dark, angry expression that crossed his face as he saw her and when she heard him fiddling about with the heavy back door which led directly out into the yard where she now stood, she realized that this was all a terrible mistake. She must have been mad. She must get away from here. She started to run towards the side of the house, hearing the door opening behind her, hearing Brad calling out, 'You again. Hey, come here!' But Ashley kept on running, not looking round, stumbling over the rough ground.

Brad caught her up, gripping her arm, forcing her round to face him. 'Don't you ever listen to anything you're told?' he barked.

She looked into his eyes. She held his look. She kept a firm check on her own emotions. She would not be angry. She loved him. If he wanted retaliation from her, then he was going to be disappointed.

'Yes.' Her voice was quiet. 'I do listen, to *everything* I'm told.'

His dark eyes narrowed. 'Am I to read something significant into that remark?' His voice was heavy with sarcasm but some of the anger had left him and Ashley was aware that he seemed unable, or unwilling, to look directly into her eyes.

'Perhaps.' Her heart was beating rapidly, but she was proud of herself for sounding much calmer than she felt.

'What?' One short word and still he would not look at her.

This was the moment. Don't back out

now, she told herself.

'Ask Milly. She knows.'

His head shot up and his eyes did lock with hers. Deep, dark brown. Wonderful eyes, if only they would shine with love for her as she knew hers were now doing for him.

'Milly? What has she got to do with it?'

Ashley smiled. Her confidence was growing. 'A great deal. Milly and I had a long talk.'

'About me? That's what you're trying to say, isn't it? You discussed me, you and my dear godmother.'

Her brand new confidence wobbled dangerously. He was not going to give her so much as an inch. But the more he dug his heels in, then the calmer she was prepared to be, at least on the surface. Calm, friendly, loving. Yes, let Bradley Thornton know she loved him. This is what Milly had told her to do. This is what she would do.

'We talked about you. Milly told me things about you,' Ashley said, as they stood there in the wild, untidy garden of Troon Manor, unaware that the thick, grey stormclouds were beginning to gather overhead, threatening rain that would, before that day was out, become a deluge that would cause havoc in Storrs and the surrounding districts; unaware, too, of the storm brewing deep inside Brad Thornton. 'She told me things she was sure of and some she guessed at, and now I'm certain of one thing, and this is that you're not the cold, hard person you pretend to be. You're only like that with me. Why, Brad? For heaven's sake, what have I ever done to you to make you act as though you hate me? We set off on the wrong foot, all right, but must we always be at loggerheads? But you don't really hate me, do you? You're miserable and I'm miserable and it's all so stupid, so let's stop it, shall we? Let's call a final truce.'

She paused for breath. It was only a

pause because she could have said much, much more. She could have mentioned the photograph of the young woman and the little boy. She was beyond caring what she said. It all had to come out so that the air could once and for all be cleared between them, but the halt to her flow of words was all Brad needed.

Again he gripped her shoulders with harsh, steely fingers. As on her last visit to Troon Island he pulled her to him and kissed her; a hard kiss; a demanding kiss without a vestige of love or tenderness in it. When he stopped kissing her he still held on to her. He spoke in a low, quiet voice, but Ashley was not deceived.

'My godmother is an interfering old busybody with nothing better to do than poke her nose into other people's business. She has always been cursed with a wild imagination and you would be wise to take anything she may have told you about me with a large handful of salt. Her speculations about me are just that.

Speculations. She doesn't know as much about me as she would like to. I don't like the idea of my private life being discussed behind my back. And let me tell you here and now, Miss Ashley Elliott, let me say once and for all that because you are a beautiful girl, because I like kissing you, because, yes, dammit, because I sometimes lie awake at night thinking about you, please don't go running away with any ridiculous ideas about me. I neither want nor need the complication of a woman in my life. Especially one whose brother-in-law belongs to the Church. I find the very thought nauseating. Run along home. Go to evensong. Say a few Hail Marys or whatever it is you Christians do for amusement. Just leave me alone. Stop pestering me. Stop badgering Milly. I'll deal with her another time.'

Finally he released her. turning abruptly and going back into the house, but not before Ashley was blinded by her tears, shaking from Brad's onslaught and cursing

181

herself and Milly too for being a couple of stupid, stupid fools.

She did not bother to analyse anything that Brad had said. He had made the final rejection. Ashley cried all the way back to the mainland, then tried to pull herself together as she sat huddled on the bus going to Storrs. On the walk back to the vicarage her tears started again, mingling now with the sudden downpour, which came on very heavy, soaking her through, running off her hair, trickling icily down her neck.

She walked slowly up the drive. She knew she should have hurried to get out of the rain, but she did not seem to have the energy. As she got to the front door it opened. Expecting Andrea with a warm welcome and perhaps some hot soup, Ashley dashed her hand across her eyes, hoping the wetness would look like rain.

A voice said, 'Ashley, love, you're like a drowned rat!' And she looked up to see Karl smiling down at her.

Ten

Karl assured Ashley that he had changed and she knew he meant it. He was softer, kinder, more considerate. He spent the whole of that day trying to convince her that he loved her, that his roving days were over and that he wanted to marry her. And she believed him. At first sight of him she had felt afraid. Why was he here? Would he be able to tell she had been crying? Apparently he did not. Nor did Andrea and Peter, who had already welcomed their surprise visitor into their home and seemed to think him likeable and charming. Of course Karl was charming. He had always gone out of his way to be so. But now his charm was no longer a sort of brittle veneer which threatened to crack at the slightest pressure, and gradually Ashley's fears subsided and she began to be glad that Karl was here. She could effectively block Brad Thornton out of her mind. He had no right to be there. He had made it painfully obvious that he did not love her, or need her, or even like her. She had best forget him as soon as she could.

And now here was Karl, looking as handsome as ever, telling her how miserable he had been, how full of remorse since that night of their blazing row when he had stormed out of her flat. He had sold some of his business ventures and bought a converted farmhouse with stables in rural Suffolk. He no longer travelled abroad as much. He intended to rear horses. And, yes, she could imagine him doing it too, even though to her knowledge he had never professed to be interested in horses. He was wearing a jacket of distinct country tweed, brown in colour, warm looking, comforting. His hand holding hers was comforting too. The love in his eyes cosseted her, enveloped her. At that moment, oh, how she needed the care and attention of someone like Karl.

He told her how he had decided he must sort himself out, put his life in order, be certain he had something stable and secure to offer her before he travelled north. And here he was. He had given no advance warning. They had communicated in no way since they had last seen one another, but by that evening he had produced the white leather box which contained a diamond solitaire ring, so beautiful, so like what Ashley would have chosen for herself. She told herself how she had once loved Karl; how only a few short months ago she would have given almost anything to have been offered such a ring by him. She told herself that here was security, a future, a man who had surely now proved his love for her. She could leave Storrs. It would be a wrench going away from Andrea and Peter, especially as their baby was so soon to be born, but they had their lives to live and she had hers. In Storrs there were too many bitter memories. She told herself she could marry Karl, hadn't she always wanted this? Wasn't this why she left London in the first place because Karl would not make any commitment to her? Well now he would, and flinging her arms around his neck she cried, 'Oh, Karl, of course I'll marry you.'

He put the ring on her finger and they went into the kitchen to tell Andrea and Peter they were engaged. There was much excitement. Peter unearthed a bottle of wine—he assured them he had not plundered the communion wine—and Andrea got out some tall-stemmed glasses. They drank a toast and Karl, so proud, so happy stood with his arm around Ashley's shoulders. But Ashley carefully avoided meeting Andrea's gaze. Her sister's eyes were too full of puzzlement, questions, despite her smiles for Karl and her words of congratulation. Andrea knew. She had always known. Later, Ashley felt sure she would have to face those questions of her sister's but not just now, and later she would have prepared herself and be able to give satisfactory answers to any questions. Now with the storm raging outside, with the gale-force winds rattling windows, ravaging trees and bushes, Ashley snuggled into the haven of Karl's arms, telling herself she was truly loved and trying so hard, so very hard not to think of Brad alone on his island.

Later, when it was all over and the extent of the damage and devastation could be viewed and assessed, the whole community was in agreement that these were the worst winter gales Storrs had ever known. But on that first wild rain-lashed night no one could tell, of course, that the rain would continue for days, that the wind would reach such a velocity as to uproot trees and demolish greenhouses, rip tiles from roofs and cause the high tides to break through the sea wall; to pound the moored boats;

to break them up and to flood the homes of so many.

On that first night it was for most only a question of lying sleepless, listening to the wind and the rain, fearing the worst, yet trying to remain optimistic that the storm would tire itself out.

Ashley was one of the sleepless but her insomnia was not due to the weather. Her mind was spinning with the events of the day. The meeting with Brad, his rejection of her; the surprise of Karl's arrival. In the darkness she touched the ring she still wore on her engagement finger. Events had moved so quickly, but wasn't that what she wanted? Soon she and Karl would be married. Their wedding would take place at St Mark's Church, of course with Peter conducting the ceremony. The four of them had talked all evening, only moving from the fireside when Andrea yawned and stretched and confessed she would go to sleep in the chair if she didn't go to bed. After Peter and Andrea had gone upstairs,

Ashley and Karl sat close together on the sofa, looking at the glowing remains of the fire.

Karl said, 'I've got my own room, of course. Much as I'd like to share yours, and besides, I want to prove to you how much I love you and that I'm willing to wait until we're married. Provided it's only a short engagement.'

Ashley kissed his cheek, liking him for what he had said. They had already decided on their wedding day so Karl would not have long to wait to share her bed, but she could not help the feeling of relief that flooded through her, and she should have listened to the warning bells because Karl was to be her husband in early January and how, after their previous intimate relationship, could she want to keep him at arm's length if she was willing to marry him? Still, it was his suggestion, not hers, but if he had wanted to ... what would she have done then? She refused to answer that question. Later,

Karl took her in his arms outside her bedroom door and kissed her fervently, but tenderly. Just such a kiss had she longed to receive from Brad Thornton, and now she responded eagerly to Karl's embrace.

'Oh, God,' he groaned, 'how am I going to find the strength to keep my hands off you?'

Ashley smiled. 'I'll help you,' she said, opening her door. 'Good-night, Karl, sleep well.'

She went quickly inside, closing the door, leaning against it, half fearing he might try to come inside. She got ready for bed, sneaking along to the bathroom only when she was certain there was no chance of meeting Karl. She had a long, hot shower, scrubbing at herself with a loofah. A ritualistic cleansing. Because of Brad? Or because of Karl? Once in her warm, cosy bed Ashley snuggled down, burying her head in the pillow, closing her eyes tightly, but sleep insisted on evading her. She felt as though her fate was sealed. Tomorrow, as soon as tomorrow, Peter would put in action the procedures that would lead to her marriage. Karl was to stay in Storrs until the wedding so necessary residency could be established. Their banns would be read out, a reception arranged—Storrs possessed one luxurious hotel set high above the main hub of the village. Ashley had often admired it and they were going to hold their reception there. Tomorrow, too, wind and weather permitting, she and Andrea were to go to Scarborough for a wedding dress and all the frills and furbelows to go with it. Andrea said she knew of a bridal boutique, small and exclusive. Very expensive too, no doubt, but what did it matter?

Tomorrow would be the 15th December. Even the approaching festive season had been overshadowed by the forthcoming wedding of Ashley Jane Elliott and Karl William Whittaker. It would not be a big wedding but Ashley knew that even a small one would not pass unnoticed in Storrs. She need only tell Milly she was engaged and within hours everybody would know. How could she tell Milly? she thought miserably. Milly, of course would tell Brad. And Brad was the last person in the world she wanted to be told anything at all about what she was doing. Ashley pushed her face into the pillow in an attempt to still her crowding thoughts. Perhaps she wouldn't say a word to Milly. Or to anyone. She and Karl could marry and leave Storrs immediately afterwards. If only they could get married sooner. Tomorrow. Ashley felt hot tears forcing themselves between her closed eyelids. If only they didn't have to marry at all ...

By morning the fierce winds seemed to have died down a little, which only served to lull the inhabitants of Storrs into a false sense of security. The rain, however, was as heavy as ever. Despite her bad night,

Ashley awoke very early and feeling quite unable to face either Andrea or Karl she got up as quickly as possible, making herself only a cup of coffee before leaving for the shop. It was most unusual for her to go there so early in the morning and she knew she was being cowardly, but she knew she needed a brief space of time alone. She left a note on the kitchen table so probably it was only a matter of time before Karl came down into the village looking for her. When he did, if he walked and he surely wouldn't use his car, he would be noticed by everyone who saw him. He would stick out like a sore thumb. Tongues would wag as all and sundry speculated about him. Once it became common knowledge that he was the fiancé of the vicar's sister-in-law there would be no stopping them. Quiet wedding or not, she and Karl would be public property. Could she face that? Could she smile and laugh and show the excitement that was expected of her as the bride-to-be of a very handsome man?

So early in the morning the village was quiet, deserted. Ashley did not even bother to lift the shop-blind or leave the door unlocked. There would be no customers. Now that she had walked from the vicarage, she realized she was hungry so she made some toast in the little kitchen which was surprisingly well equipped, and brewed another mug of strong coffee. She shivered in the chill morning air, and hurried to plug in the fan-heater, which was generally quite adequate.

Through the glass panels on the door the murk and gloom of the December morning lingered and rain was spattering on the glass. The morning matched Ashley's mood. But once she had eaten the toast and the little shop had become warm and cosy she felt better. This was her haven. Here she felt safe; surrounded by books, toys, magazines, knick-knacks. All the things she had grown to love. It hit her then that she would have to give the shop up. How could she? She moved around touching items here and there. She belonged here. She belonged in Storrs. Even without Brad she belonged. Oh, how could she leave? How could she marry Karl and go away? And how could she deceive him into thinking she loved him when Brad Thornton had possession of her heart?

She looked at her ring. It was lovely but she didn't deserve it. Now in the early morning light she could think quietly and rationally, for the first time since she had seen Karl standing on the doorstep. She must not make Karl suffer because of Brad. Karl loved her, he had offered her marriage. He had done all he could to prove his change of heart towards her, but it wasn't enough. It could never be enough.

The bell above the door jingled and Ashley looked up, startled to see Brad coming in. He wore a dark trenchcoat, with turned-up collar and a flat cap pulled on to his head. He stood, taking up all the doorway.

'I'm not open,' Ashley said coldly, though she did not feel cold as the warm rush of her love and longing for him suffused her being.

'I know. I've not come to buy anything.'

'How did you get in?' she asked. When he showed her his key she remembered she had taken the spare one from him. Only Milly still had a key. Had he come from Milly?

'I've come to take you away from here.' Brad's voice was low and serious.

Ashley swallowed hard, keeping the counter's width between them.

'What do you mean?' she demanded. 'Take me where? Perhaps you ought to know that I'm getting married.'

He gave a brief nod. 'Yes, so I heard. Well, I won't bother offering my congratulations. They won't be necessary.' He moved further into the shop.

'How did you hear? I haven't told anybody yet.'

'It doesn't matter. Get your coat, you're coming with me.'

All her instincts screamed at her to do as he said; to grab her coat and leave the shop with him; to go with him wherever he wanted her to. But common sense prevailed. It was a trick. She had no reason to trust him.

'Don't tell me what to do,' she snapped. Why have you come here, Brad? What's the real reason? Didn't you say everything you wanted to say to me yesterday morning?'

He took off his cap, shaking the rain from it, rubbing his hand across his face to remove some of the wet.

'Yesterday?' he repeated in an odd, almost wistful way. 'Was it only yesterday? It seems a lifetime ago.'

He was acting strangely. Gone was his hardness, his sarcasm. He seemed dazed, unsure of himself and Ashley now noticed he was unshaven; he looked tired too, worn out in fact. As though he had gone a night without sleep.

Softly she ventured, 'Would ... would you like some tea?'

'What?' It was as though he was having a real effort to concentrate.

'Tea. Would you like some?'

'Perhaps I would. Thank you.'

Ashley scarcely dared breathe. Could it be that for the first time they were behaving normally towards each other? Being friendly; polite. Now ... when it was too late. When she wore Karl's ring on her finger. When Brad—how, she did not know—had already heard of her engagement.

As she turned towards the little kitchen he came up at the back of her, so swiftly she was unaware he had moved. From behind he folded his arms around her, holding her tightly, making her gasp with the suddenness and strength of his hold on her.

'Are you going to come quietly or are

we going to do it the hard way?' His voice was no longer uncertain, but strong, demanding.

Ashley could not move. She felt a little shiver of fear. No, not fear. How could she fear this man she loved so much? It was more of a thrill—an eager anticipation as to what he would do next.

Unable to turn and look at him, she shook her head swiftly to and fro.

'I won't come with you!' she cried. 'Why should I? Let me go, you're hurting me. What's the matter with you? Have you gone crazy?'

'Yes, crazy. Because of you, Ashley Elliott. Oh, what's the use of talking? We can't talk here and I know you won't come willingly so, here goes.' With one swift movement he had twisted her round, still holding her. As she opened her mouth to speak she saw that he was grinning, actually grinning. Then he said, 'Blame Milly, darling, she said I had to stop at nothing. But I apologize in advance!'

His right hand moved but by the time Ashley realized what he was going to do with his gently clenched fist it was too late. He bopped her on the chin, not hard but very effectively. For the first time in her life, Ashley realized the expression 'to see stars' was no exaggeration.

Eleven

There was a pain in her head and an even worse one in her jaw and when she rubbed it she winced. Her eyes flickered open. She was lying on the floor on a mattress, covered by a blanket. She could feel the warmth of the fire which burned and crackled in the enormous fireplace in front of which she lay. She tried to collate her thoughts. Where was she? The room was dim but not dark so it wasn't night-time. The wind was howling against the uncurtained windows, making them rattle and rain ran down them in rivers. It was a big room but held no furniture except an old wooden bedstead minus mattress, which was probably the one she was lying on.

When another wince of pain shot through

her jaw, Ashley remembered. Brad had hit her! Knocked her out, so he must have brought her here and 'here' was ... ? Where else could it be but Troon Island and this was one of the empty dirty rooms of the neglected Manor House. In a nutshell, she had been kidnapped!

The remembrance should have terrified her, sent her scurrying for the door in a bid for freedom. It did nothing of the sort, but only caused her to turn on her side with a contented sigh and gaze happily into the fire. Because she had remembered something else. Brad had called her 'darling'. The sock on the jaw meant nothing. Hadn't he said he was sorry, and implied he had no other choice? She did not know or care how he had found out about her and Karl, but only that he had seen fit to take her, by force if necessary, away from Storrs and either by boat or car to Troon Island. There could be only one reason for such outrageous behaviour. Bradley Thornton loved her!

The idea made her heart sing. The door opened and he came in, crossing to her and setting down a tray containing steaming mugs of coffee, a plate of chocolate biscuits and slices of thickly buttered malt loaf, rich and dark and most appetizing to look at. His smile for her was as warm as her inner glow.

'Sorry it isn't exactly a feast,' he said.

Looking into his eyes Ashley replied, 'To me it is.' She picked up a piece of malt loaf and bit into it, feeling the warm rich taste of the butter on her lips.

'And I'm even sorrier this isn't the Ritz, but it's the best I can do for you.' He knelt down beside her and gently touched her face. 'Does it hurt?'

'A bit. Not much.'

'There's a bruise, I'm afraid.'

'It doesn't matter,' Ashley assured him, 'but the reason you did it does. I've got thousands of questions I want to ask you; it's just knowing where to begin.'

Brad picked up his mug of coffee. 'Take

all the time you want. We'll be here for some time.' He nodded towards the window. 'The causeway's closed till this storm abates and I daren't use the boat. In fact, my cottage is off-limits. That's why I brought you up here. If the sea gets any rougher there's a real danger of flooding.'

Ashley sat hugging her knees, looking at the fire. 'How did you get me here?'

'By car. I just made it though the car is somewhat waterlogged. I'd a feeling we were going to be marooned. The weather forecasts were horrendous, but we won't starve, I've brought as much as I could up from the cottage. We won't die of cold either. And the house still has all mains services.'

'Sounds heavenly,' Ashley sighed, 'but why are you so nice to me all of a sudden? Yesterday ...'

He stopped her with a soft gentle kiss.

'Yesterday I was a bloody fool, as I've been ever since I picked you up from those rocks, but thank God I came to my senses just in time. With Milly's help, of course. I wouldn't care to repeat some of the names she called me.'

'Did Milly know about Karl and me?'

'Yes. Your sister phoned her very early this morning. Apparently she heard you getting up, came down and saw your note. She knew, wise woman, that you didn't love Karl, but that you did love me.' Brad paused, taking hold of her hand, stroking a finger along her palm in a very sensuous way. 'You do love me, don't you, Ashley? I'm not still making a bloody fool of myself, am I?'

'Yes, I love you.' Ashley's voice was dreamy, then feeling her senses heightening, very much aware she was lying in front of a good fire on a mattress, albeit a rather dirty one, she pulled her hand free and said sharply, 'Though why I should, heaven only knows!'

But she wasn't really cross and Brad knew she wasn't. For a few moments they were silent, content, each with their own thoughts, listening to the storm outside, glad of their safe haven.

Ashley saw the glitter of the engagement ring Karl had given her, and removed it, putting it in the pocket of her jeans. If Brad saw her do it, he did not remark on it but said, 'Milly told me I had to tell you everything. Until last night even she didn't know the whole truth, but I went to her after you'd left the island. She refused me any sympathy until I came clean with her. She upbraided me in no uncertain terms for the way I had treated you.'

Ashley could not refrain from saying, 'Hadn't she done so before? You didn't take any notice of her, did you?'

'No, I didn't. I loved you. I loved you as soon as I saw you. I couldn't help myself. It was such an overwhelming feeling. My heart told me to gather you into my arms and never let you go.'

Ashley looked at him. 'Then why didn't you?'

'Fair question. And I'll try to answer it, by telling you about myself, that is, the parts you haven't already heard from Milly.' He grinned. 'I understand she's told you plenty.'

He sat by her on the mattress, holding her in the crook of his arm. She rested her head against him. Now she knew without a doubt that he never would let her go.

'I was married to an Italian girl. She was eighteen when we married and I was twenty. I'd been living in Italy for two years when I met Luisa and we were very much in love. When I heard about my father's death, we already had a little boy, Paul, he was just two years old.'

Ashley remembered the picture. Luisa and Paul. Brad's wife and baby son. She waited breathlessly to hear what had happened to them.

Brad went on. 'We set off in great excitement, travelling by car. I was a bit apprehensive about taking the baby on such a journey, but Luisa was so looking forward to visiting England that I could not leave her behind. You might think I sound rather callous, not being too upset about my father's death, but we'd never been close. I hadn't seen or heard from him for over four years. Well, now Troon Island and the Manor House were mine, though very neglected I'd been told. We didn't mind. We were young, enthusiastic, we had all the time in the world ...' He paused and when he spoke again, Ashley heard the bitterness in his voice; she twisted in his arms and pulled him close, to protect him, to try to ease his pain as he told her what had happened.

'We planned to motor through Austria and France. Taking it easy. Making several stops along the way. I was working as a freelance photographer then so could more or less please myself about what I did with my time. We got as far as the Austrian border. Just past Vipiteno. Have you ever seen the Europa Bridge, Ashley? I don't suppose you have. Neither had Luisa. An Italian born and bred but her horizons were very limited. She was a sweet, simple girl and I was going to give her the earth.'

He was torturing himself, but Ashley knew it had to come out. Then maybe he could rid himself of the bitterness for ever.

'There was an accident. A car coming in the opposite direction ploughed straight into us. I had no warning. He came straight across the road. It would have been a head-on collision if I hadn't taken evasive action. But I did and I crashed into a wall. I wasn't hurt except for a broken ankle and various cuts and bruises, but Luisa in the front passenger seat and Paul in his baby seat in the back were both killed instantly.' Brad looked at her. She could hardly bear to face him. Still the bitterness was there. In his eyes. In his grim, unsmiling mouth. 'The driver of the other car escaped without a scratch. He was a priest, Ashley. A Roman Catholic priest; and he was drunk. Very, very drunk. Because of him I lost my wife and my baby.'

So that was why he hated the Church and made so many disparaging remarks about Peter.

'Oh, Brad, my darling!' She covered his wet face with kisses and for a while they wept together. 'I'm so sorry.'

'I know it wasn't your fault and yet I wanted to blame you because your brother-in-law was a vicar,' Brad said. 'And even before I knew that, whilst you were still unconscious on my boat I steeled myself against you because for the first time since losing Luisa, I had met somebody who stirred me, who disturbed me. I sat watching you, just watching you, holding your hand, but, of course, you didn't know that. I thought of my feelings for you as a weakness. A weakness I had to fight and overcome. I didn't want to love again. I didn't want to be hurt again.'

'You won't be,' Ashley promised him fervently.

'Each time I met you it got worse. I wanted so much to be able to tell you I loved you, but I couldn't. I'd lived so long with bitterness and hatred for that priest and for the Church he represented, any church, and though I loved you, I hated you too, for getting under my skin, for making me think of you in that way. It seemed disloyal to Luisa's memory.'

'And now?'

A smile came at last. 'Now, I know I can remember both Luisa and Paul with love. I know I need never forget them, but I need never feel guilty either because of my love for you.'

'I'm still a vicar's sister-in-law,' Ashley reminded him.

'He seems a decent enough fellow, what I've seen of him,' Brad admitted, 'and he's well thought of in Storrs. Now don't go running away with the idea that I'll start going to church, because I won't, but

I might be generous and marry you in church if that's what you want.'

She pretended to be surprised. 'Marry me? But I hardly know you!'

His smile now was slow and sensuous. 'We'll have plenty of time to remedy that,' he told her. 'We might be here for days. So far as I know there's only one bed in the whole house.'

'You mean that one?' Ashley pointed with feigned disgust at the wooden bedstead.

Brad shrugged his shoulders. 'I could perhaps find some decent sheets and things. I've got some warming through very nicely, thank you, in the airing cupboard.'

'Were you expecting company?'

'I was.'

'What about poor Karl?' Ashley was struck by a sudden twinge of conscience.

'I think he'll have got the message by now, my love.'

Another thought struck her. 'Tell me something, Brad,' she said, 'have you been working on the house?'

His glance was innocent. 'What makes you think that?'

'I saw you with that wheelbarrow full of rubbish. I just wondered.'

He kissed her full on the mouth. 'It was good therapy for me. I've hardly begun to scratch the surface of what needs to be done, but it *will* get done. All of it, I promise you. And we'll live here one day. You and I. And our children.'

His mouth trembled as he said this and Ashley took hold of his hand and gave it a squeeze.

'And in the meantime there's always your cottage,' she said.

'Provided it doesn't get swept out to sea.'

They both turned to contemplate the vile weather outside the windows. Ashley knew she should be worrying about the people in Storrs, about Andrea, Peter and Milly, and yes, about Karl, but just now she wanted to think of nothing but being with Brad and how much she loved him. Tomorrow would be time enough for worrying. What was left of today belonged to her and Brad.

In the pale light of a wet and windswept dawn, Ashley awoke from a deep, refreshing sleep. Immediately she was aware of a sense of peace and satisfaction. The weather outside did not seem to have improved much and today she knew she would have to face an awkward situation and give an explanation, but none of that worried her. She had her allies. Andrea and Milly would back her up, perhaps have already eased the way with Karl. Perhaps Peter, too, would not be too disapproving of what had happened. Today, too, there may be flood, storm and tempest to encounter. Ashley knew that Brad had hoped for a worsening in the weather so that they could be marooned for longer, but last night she had finally got him to admit that during daylight hours he would be willing to take the boat out if she really insisted, and she did insist. She had to. She would spend the rest of her life with Brad. She had to be fair to Karl. To face him. To return his ring. She wasn't looking forward to it, but it had to be done.

Now, however, she stretched luxuriously before settling down to another hour or two's sleep. She snuggled up under the covers as close to Brad's warm back as she could get. Her movements roused him slightly so that he murmured in his sleep and flung out his arm across her. She saw his outstretched fingers and noticed something she had not seen before. On his little finger he wore a small silver ring; a ring with two intertwined fishes. A ring identical to the one she had bought from Milly's shop. How long ago that seemed now!

If she had known Brad possessed an identical ring, obviously bought from Milly's shop, as hers was, Ashley would never have doubted that one day they would belong to one another.

The publishers hope that this book has given you enjoyable reading. Large Print Books are especially designed to be as easy to see and hold as possible. If you wish a complete list of our books, please ask at your local library or write direct to: Ulverscroft Large Print Books Limited, Anstey, Leicestershire, LE7 7FU, England.

This Large Print Book for the Partially sighted, who cannot read normal print, is published under the auspices of

THE ULVERSCROFT FOUNDATION

THE ULVERSCROFT FOUNDATION

. . . we hope that you have enjoyed this Large Print Book. Please think for a moment about those people who have worse eyesight problems than you . . . and are unable to even read or enjoy Large Print, without great difficulty.

You can help them by sending a donation, large or small to:

**The Ulverscroft Foundation,
1, The Green, Bradgate Road,
Anstey, Leicestershire, LE7 7FU,
England.**

or request a copy of our brochure for more details.

The Foundation will use all your help to assist those people who are handicapped by various sight problems and need special attention.

Thank you very much for your help.

Other DALES Romance Titles In Large Print

RUTH ABBEY
House By The Tarn

MARGARET BAUMANN
Firefly

NANCY BUCKINGHAM
Romantic Journey

HILDA PERRY
A Tower Of Strength

IRENE LAWRENCE
Love Rides The Skies

HILDA DURMAN
Under The Apple Blossom

Other DALES Romance Titles
In Large Print